Miss Wrench mounted the platform look... grim-faced. She omitted her usual greeting and began addressing the school in a sombre voice.

'Today is a sad day for Redwood. The structures of the main building, along with the girls' wing, have been officially classed as dangerous. Subsidence is so substantial that it would take a quarter of a million pounds to put it right.' She paused, struggling to keep her voice under control. 'A quarter of a million pounds that the school doesn't have.'

Cassie listened intently to the Principal's next words. There was not a sound in the hall except Miss Wrench's flat, tired-sounding voice.

'The girls' wing has already been evacuated, but we can only go on using the main building for a matter of weeks. After that, Redwood Ballet School must close.'

The Ballet School series

Stars of the Ballet School

Mal Lewis Jones

Hodder
Children's
Books

a division of Hodder Headline plc

Children for cover illustration by courtesy of Gaston Payne
School of Theatre, Dance and Drama.

Special thanks to Freed of London Ltd., 94 St Martins Lane,
London WC2N for the loan of dancewear

First published in Great Britain in 1995
by Hodder Children's Books

A Catalogue record for this book is available from the British Library

ISBN 0 340 60734 3

Typeset by Avon Dataset Ltd, Bidford-on-Avon

Printed and bound in Great Britain by
Cox & Wyman Ltd, Reading, Berks.

Hodder Children's Books
A Division of Hodder Headline plc
338 Euston Road
London NW1 3BH

Contents

1

Another Birthday Party

Cassie Brown looked at herself in the wardrobe mirror with a new feeling of confidence. Nothing had really changed in her appearance; she was still brown-haired, brown-eyed, with that irritating gap between her front teeth. But she *felt* different. The tour of France with her ballet school, from which she had just returned, had done that for her.

She had spent her thirteenth birthday abroad, and been given the unexpected chance to dance the leading role in *Cinderella*. On top of that, she and her friends had found themselves caught up in an exciting, sometimes terrifying, mystery.

Coping with all these new experiences far away

from home had made Cassie feel much older and tougher.

But that didn't mean she couldn't still enjoy childhood treats. Her parents had invited her best friends – Becky, Emily and Poppy – to their home for the day, to celebrate Cassie's birthday in the traditional Brown family style. They were going to stay overnight and be driven back to school the next day with Cassie.

As she dressed, the delicious smell of her birthday cake cooking in the kitchen downstairs wafted up to her room. There was nothing like her mum's birthday cakes – not even the beautiful one prepared for her in the kitchens of the Paris Ballet School could compare.

Cassie had been tired for the three days she'd already spent at home. But now, having caught up on her sleep, she felt full of energy and bursting to see her friends, who should be arriving very soon.

She was especially looking forward to seeing Emily, who had been recovering from anorexia, and had had to miss the tour.

Eating a late breakfast in the kitchen, Cassie chatted to her mum about the tour and the planned birthday tea.

'I've got a video for you girls to watch after tea,' said Joy Brown.

'Thanks, Mum,' said Cassie. 'Where's Dad by the way?'

'He's gone off to a meeting,' she said.

'What, in the Easter holidays?'

2

Joy laughed. 'A teacher's job doesn't automatically stop at the end of term, you know.' Her face grew serious. 'Your father's got a lot on his plate at the moment.'

'I thought he seemed quiet,' said Cassie. 'What's the matter then?'

'The numbers on the school roll have dropped a bit and they're talking again about closing it down.'

'Oh, that would be awful!' Cassie had fond memories of her little village Primary School.

'Yes, it would,' agreed Joy. 'A great loss to the village.'

'But what can Dad do?'

'He can fight,' answered Joy. 'Your father, the other teachers and some of the parents are going to do their utmost to see that the school isn't closed down.'

'Glad to hear it,' said Cassie, with a twinge of pride for her dad.

'Now you're up, you can help me make up the camp beds for your friends.'

'OK Mum, but I don't think there will be room for all of them in my room.'

'No, you're right. One can go in your room and the other two will have to sleep in the bunk beds in Rachel's room.'

'That will be great. I'll have Emily with me, and Becky and Poppy can go in the bunks.'

The arrangement seemed ideal. It would give Cassie a chance to talk to Emily about how she was getting on with her family since her father had returned to them. Emily was always a very private person, and might not feel able to speak openly while the others were about. On the phone, she had sounded very positive and Cassie felt hopeful that her anorexia had been cured.

After the beds had been prepared, Cassie could find nothing to do. She was restless, waiting for her friends to arrive.

Poppy was the first to roll up outside the door. She had come straight from Redwood Ballet School, and had had the shortest journey. Her home was in Australia so she spent short holidays at the boarding-school.

Cassie rushed down the drive to welcome her red-haired friend, and Miss Eiseldown, their house-mother, who had driven her down.

It seems odd to have Miss Eiseldown in our kitchen, sipping coffee and talking to Mum, Cassie thought. School and home were usually such separate worlds.

'The tour went very well, I hear,' said Miss Eiseldown.

'Yes, it was great,' said Cassie, 'but I can't wait to get back to school.'

'Oh *someone's* keen!' Miss Eiseldown exclaimed to Joy Brown.

'I don't think anything would stop Cassie dancing now,' laughed Joy.

'I don't know – breaking both her legs might do the trick!' joked Poppy.

Miss Eiseldown made a hasty exit when Mr and Mrs Hastings arrived with Becky a few minutes later. The house-mother had met Mrs Hastings before. But

4

Becky's mother collared her in the hall.

'Oh, Miss Eiseldown, *so* nice to see you again. I was hoping you'd tell us all about the tour and how Becky did in her part. Such a shame we couldn't have been there to watch ourselves. Still, I imagine the performances were absolutely lovely!'

'I, er, didn't actually go on the tour myself, Mrs Hastings,' Miss Eiseldown managed to say. 'I had to stay at Redwood with the children who couldn't go home for the holidays.'

'Oh yes, how silly of me!'

'I really must be going now,' said Miss Eiseldown, trying to move past Mrs Hastings.

'Well, perhaps you could tell us instead, as Becky's house-mother, how her dancing is coming on. Will she make it, do you think?'

'I really couldn't comment on Becky's dancing. I teach her mathematics,' said Miss Eiseldown. 'Now, if you'll excuse me . . .' Becky's father took pity on the young teacher and backed down the hall to let her pass.

Once Cassie had waved off her house-mother, she took her two friends upstairs to her bedroom, leaving her mother to entertain Becky's parents.

'I've done nothing but sleep since I got home,' said Cassie, bouncing down on her bed. 'How about you?'

'I was pretty tired the first day back,' said Becky, brushing her long, ash-blonde hair back from her face. 'But I've spent a lot of time with the animals these last couple of days.'

'I was having a nap on my bed the first day,' said

Poppy, 'when this strange man came barging into our room without any warning. He frightened me to death!'

'Who was he?' asked Cassie.

'I don't really know,' said Poppy. 'He didn't know anyone was in our room, I suppose. I've seen him about quite a lot since then, taking measurements and wandering about outside the building.'

'Well, it does sound as though he's got some business being at Redwood, at least,' said Cassie. 'I wonder what's going on, though?'

Poppy shrugged. 'Perhaps they think we're too squashed and are planning to extend the girls' wing?'

'I shouldn't think that's very likely,' laughed Becky. She was sitting next to the window, which overlooked the lane. 'A car's just pulled up. I wonder if it's Emily?'

'I can't wait to see her,' said Cassie, rushing to the window. 'I wonder if she's fully recovered.'

'Well let's hope so,' said Becky. 'She certainly gave us all a fright last term.'

When Emily joined them a few minutes later, the friends could see that she looked very well indeed. The gaunt cheeks and dark rings under her eyes had disappeared. Now her light brown hair shone, her eyes sparkled and even her skin had a healthy bloom to it.

After hugging everyone, Emily demanded to hear all about the tour. There was so much to tell her that they were still noisily discussing it when Joy called them down for tea.

All Cassie's favourite foods were on the table, but

as she sat down ready to tuck in, Cassie suddenly became anxious for Emily. Perhaps she would refuse to eat, or just nibble something out of politeness. Her fears were groundless, however; Emily ate with as big an appetite as anyone. Cassie relaxed and enjoyed her tea-party, delighted to see Emily really was cured.

Joy brought in the birthday cake on a silver stand. She had decorated the cake with chocolate icing and a perfect pair of pink ballet shoes.

'I can't believe you're a teenager,' said Joy lighting the thirteen candles.

'Nor can I,' laughed Cassie. 'There are too many candles now to blow out in one go!'

Unintentionally, Becky was handed the largest slice of cake. 'Ooh, this is really yummy,' she said, and readily accepted a second piece.

The girls went for a stroll after tea, down the country lane which ran in front of the Brown's cottage. The weather had turned warm and they were glad to be outside without jackets. It was Emily's turn to tell her news. Her family problems seemed to have improved remarkably now her father had come back. She didn't go into details, but Cassie could see that she felt far happier with the new situation, and was glad for her.

'I suppose you've been reading masses of books while you've been recuperating?' asked Becky.

'A few,' said Emily, 'but after a while I got fed up with reading and watching television.'

'Whatever did you do then?' asked Cassie, who knew Emily must have felt terribly frustrated at not being able to dance at all.

'I practised my flute,' said Emily.

The other three looked at one another and Emily giggled. 'Don't look so shocked!' she said. 'I'm really enjoying it. I'll play you something I've learned with Dad, when we get back to the house.'

Emily kept her promise and played them the new piece. At the end of it, her friends burst into applause.

'That was wonderful, Emily!' cried Cassie. 'But I don't remember you ever playing like that before. And the piece was far harder too!'

Emily smiled; a glow had lit her face.

'I've spent hour after hour practising and Dad's helped me a lot – he plays the flute, you know. I'm really hooked now!'

Cassie guessed that the flute had probably drawn father and daughter closer together, which was just what Emily had needed.

It was something of a shock to get back into the school routine the next day. Thankfully, lessons didn't begin until the day after. All the students had to be weighed and measured and passed as medically fit.

Cassie passed Ojo, limping out of the medical room.

'How did you get on?' she asked.

Ojo shrugged. 'They're going to give me physio, but I'm not allowed to dance for another four to six weeks.'

'How awful!' said Cassie. Ojo had pulled tendons in his right leg on the French tour, and had been unable to continue dancing the part of the Prince in *Cinderella*.

'I'm going to be so fed up,' he complained.

Cassie remembered the time she'd sprained her ankle. 'It'll pass quickly, Ojo,' she reassured him. 'Just go to all the classes. It's surprising what you can pick up just by watching!'

'I'm going to get behind, whatever I do,' said Ojo.

'You'll catch up again, you'll see!' Cassie said brightly, but she recalled vividly how frustrating it had been not to be able to join in classes.

Cassie then spotted Jane, looking very miserable.

'Whatever's the matter with you?' asked Cassie.

'My assessment letter was waiting for me when I got home,' she answered in a very quiet voice.

'Oh, Jane, surely they're not chucking you out?'

'Afraid so, Cassie. There's five of us going altogether.'

'That's awful. I didn't think they'd bother so much at the end of the second year. What are you going to do?'

'Well, I'm seeing this term out, though it's going to be really hard with everyone knowing I've failed to get into the third year.'

'Don't worry, Jane. We're all on your side!'

'And Miss Wrench is going to fix up some auditions for me at other schools. Mum and Dad are willing to pay fees, fortunately. But I really don't want to leave . . .'

Cassie could see Jane was trying hard not to cry. She suggested they made their way to the dining-hall for lunch.

Cassie rejoined her friends at their table, next to a

deep sash window and told them about Jane.

'I wonder why they're not keeping her on?' said Poppy. 'She seems perfectly fine in all her classes.'

'I don't know,' said Cassie. 'It may be something to do with the way her body's coping with the dancing. They take a lot of notice of the medical experts, don't they?' She sighed. 'It's quite a strain, wondering how you're going to grow and develop.'

'Yes,' agreed Becky. 'Any hint of knock-knees and you might as well give up!'

They all giggled. 'Do you know, I've grown another two centimetres since last term?' said Cassie. 'I'm going to end up being too tall for a dancer, I know I am!'

'Well if the worst comes to the worst, you'll make a good model,' teased Emily.

'I don't want to be a model!' cried Cassie horrified. 'Sitting around in ridiculous fashion clothes!'

'I wouldn't mind,' said Poppy. 'It looks quite a glamorous life.'

'Mind you,' said Emily, 'dancing looks glamorous, to the spectator, but we know what hard work it is, don't we?'

'Look!' cried Poppy suddenly, pointing at something outside the window. 'There's that man again!'

'What man?' asked Cassie, following her gaze.

'The man who burst into my room!'

The man in question seemed to be setting up surveying equipment in the grounds, not far from the dining-hall. Cassie could see him quite clearly.

10

He was short, clean-shaven, sandy-haired and looked about thirty.

'He hasn't gone away then,' she said. 'Perhaps we ought to go outside and investigate. Everyone finished eating?'

'I think I'm going to have seconds,' said Becky. 'You go without me.'

'Count me out,' said Emily. 'I've got some flute practice to do.'

So Cassie and Poppy went outside on their own. They tried to look casual as they strolled up to the surveyor.

'What does that instrument do?' asked Cassie, trying to strike up a conversation with him.

'Haven't got time to answer stupid questions,' he answered abruptly. He picked up his equipment and turned on his heel.

It took Cassie a few moments to recover from her surprise. 'Some people!' she exclaimed.

'That's what he was like with me,' said Poppy. 'Never even had the manners to say sorry for barging in on me.'

As the girls wandered back into the school, Cassie wondered what on earth the ill-mannered surveyor was doing at Redwood.

2

Mrs Allingham's Costumes

'I feel as if I've been back at school for weeks, not just one night!' said Cassie with a yawn.

The girls had just come out of their ballet class with Miss Oakland. She had worked them very hard, correcting tiny errors that had been creeping into their exercises on the tour.

Pulling out the hair-grips which were securing the plaits on top of her head, Cassie noticed Celia talking to Jane, out of the corner of her eye. Jane was painfully shy, so Celia didn't usually bother with her.

Cassie turned and looked more closely. Though she couldn't hear what Celia was actually saying above the general hubbub of the changing-room, she could see that Jane was very close to tears.

'I wonder what Celia's been saying to her?' said Cassie aloud, but really to herself.

'What?' asked Becky, but Cassie had already drifted over to find out for herself. She just caught the tail end of Celia gloating over Jane's failure to secure a place at Redwood for the third year.

'I'm not the only one,' said Jane, unable to stem the tears. 'There's Melissa and Audrey and . . .'

'Bet your parents are pretty cross,' Celia cut in.

'Oh, Celia!' intervened Cassie. 'Stop rubbing it in.'

'I'm not,' retorted Celia. 'I was just offering a shoulder to cry on, wasn't I, Jane?'

Jane sniffed into her hanky, but didn't reply. Cassie turned to her.

'Well, if she gives you any more bother, let me know,' she said, glaring at Celia.

'Huh,' scoffed Celia. 'And what would you be able to do about it?'

'I'll think of something,' said Cassie. 'Now why don't you leave Jane alone while she gets changed? We're all going to be late as it is.'

'Thanks, Cassie,' breathed Jane, when Celia had moved away. 'It's bad enough just thinking about leaving Redwood, without being made to look a fool.'

'Just walk off if she tries it again,' said Cassie, 'and come and see me.'

Jane tagged along with Cassie all through break, afraid that Celia might pick on her again.

They wandered through the grounds nearest the school buildings, munching doughnuts.

14

'Wasn't that surveyor rude last night?' said Poppy.

'He was,' agreed Cassie. 'I'd love to know what he's doing here.'

As the girls rounded the corner of their wing, they all stopped in surprise.

Several workmen were erecting scaffolding against the longest wall of the wing. Directing operations was the sandy-haired surveyor.

'There must be some repair work going on,' said Becky.

'I wish we could find out more,' said Cassie, 'but there's no point asking him, is there?'

The surveyor had glanced in their direction and Cassie could tell by the set of his jaw that he wasn't pleased to see them.

'I think we'd better make ourselves scarce,' said Cassie. 'He can't be here all the time. We'll come back later.'

The friends could see nothing of the scaffolding from the various classrooms they sat in during the rest of the school day. Even the dining-hall overlooked the wrong side of the grounds.

But when it was preparation time, just before supper, the girls were able to go up to Room 12 and gaze out of the window at the work in progress.

The surveyor still seemed to be overseeing the work. As they watched, he approached one of the workmen – a skinny, sad-faced chap – and started speaking to him.

The pair were directly under the girls' window. Cassie edged the sash window up a little, so they

15

could overhear the conversation.

The surveyor had raised his voice. He seemed to be complaining about the length of time it had taken the workmen to put up the scaffolding. The skinny man was apologetic, but the surveyor carried on angrily.

Cassie shut the window. 'Phew!' she said. 'I think I've heard enough!'

'What a horrible man!' said Becky.

The girls felt unable to return to their chatter, with the surveyor's curses still ringing in their ears.

'I don't know whether it's having that man about,' announced Cassie after a few moments, 'but I think there's a funny atmosphere in the school since we got back.'

'I agree,' said Poppy. 'I noticed it even before you lot came.'

'Can't say I have,' said Becky. 'The food's as bad as ever. What's changed?'

'Little things,' said Cassie. 'None of the teachers look particularly happy. Usually after a holiday, they're full of energy.'

'Yes,' said Emily. 'At least, they normally start off cheerful!'

'And did you notice Miss Wrench in assembly?' asked Cassie.

'She looked her usual smiling self to me,' said Becky.

'Well, I know she always scowls,' said Cassie, 'but she was different today – as though she had other things on her mind.'

'It can't be an easy job, though, can it, being head

of a school like this?' asked Emily.

Cassie's mind drifted to her father, who had his own school troubles. She started to feel uneasy.

'Let's nip out,' she suggested.

'I don't fancy bumping into that surveyor fellow again,' said Emily.

Cassie peered out of the window. 'I think he's gone. In fact, the workmen are packing up too. Let's be quick.'

The four girls abandoned their homework, and let themselves out of the back door of the wing. They were just in time to catch the skinny chap who had caught the worst end of the surveyor's tongue.

'Excuse me,' Cassie said, smiling sweetly. 'We couldn't help noticing you were putting up scaffolding all round our wing.'

'That's right, miss,' said the workman. 'Should finish by tomorrow.'

'Er – could you tell us what it's for?' asked Cassie.

'No, not really. Haven't been told.'

'Oh.' Cassie looked disappointed. 'That man in charge doesn't seem very friendly. He wouldn't talk to us yesterday.'

'The boss,' he said. 'No, he's not a friendly chappy, that he isn't.'

'Have you known him long?'

'The boss? No – first time I've worked for him.'

'What's his name?' asked Cassie

'Smithson,' said the skinny workman. 'But that's about all I knows about him.'

Her curiosity still afire, Cassie had to be content

17

with the few crumbs she had gleaned so far.

The next day, rehearsals got under way for the end of year Gala. It was to include a shortened version of *Cinderella*, along with a variety of short pieces, ranging from tap to jazz ballet.

Madame was in charge of the first rehearsal, in which the students ran through *Cinderella*, with the new cuts explained. Tom still danced the role of the Prince, which he had taken over on tour, when Ojo had had his accident on stage. Cassie, who had taken the female lead on the very last night of the tour, was not so lucky; Miss Wrench had promised Emily that she would dance Cinderella if she got better for the summer term.

Cassie didn't mind. She'd had her moment of glory in France. Now it was her friend's turn to enjoy a much-deserved chance of being in the limelight. She was quite content to return to her lovely solo as the Spring Fairy.

But Celia was not so happy at losing the Spring Fairy part to Cassie. When the girls spilled out into the changing-room after the rehearsal, Cassie could hear Celia complaining bitterly about it to Abigail. As Cassie passed her, she turned her back pointedly.

Cassie walked quickly over to Emily, Becky and Poppy.

'Celia's in a mood,' she said to her friends.

'What's new?' said Becky.

'I'm still really cross with her for going on at Jane,' Cassie said.

'Celia's not very good at considering other people's

feelings – only her own,' agreed Poppy.

The conversation didn't seem to reach Emily. She was in a little world of her own.

'I can't believe it,' Emily said suddenly.

'Oh, I could believe anything of Celia,' said Poppy.

'Celia?' asked Emily looking mystified. 'No, I just can't believe I'll be dancing Cinderella in July. It's like a dream come true.'

Cassie smiled warmly, showing her dimples. 'You're going to make a beautiful Cinderella. You did so well today, and it's only your first rehearsal.'

'Thanks, Cassie,' said Emily. 'You and Abigail are going to be hard acts to follow. I'm glad it's going to be a different audience.'

Cassie's mind went back to her own performance of the part – her first leading role – and how wonderful the experience had been. Becky's voice broke into her thoughts.

'Shall we go across to Mrs Allingham's in the lunch-hour? I want to see if Tinker's all right.'

The others agreed. It was a fine day for a walk across the grounds to the little cottage where their elderly friend lived. And so, after hurriedly eating their lasagne and apple crumble, the four friends trekked over the lawns and through the wilder area near the woods by the boundary wall.

Mrs Allingham was sitting outside in a garden-chair when they arrived. Becky was delighted to find Tinker curled up on her lap, purring loudly. The other kitten was fast asleep under the old lady's chair.

'Haven't they grown!' exclaimed Becky, after the

girls and Mrs Allingham had exchanged greetings. She scooped Tinker up in her arms and held him to her. He was still purring like a lawn-mower.

'Well, I'm delighted to see you girls,' said Mrs Allingham. 'Give me a hand to get out of this wretched chair, Cassandra and I'll fetch you something to drink.'

'No really, don't worry,' said Cassie. 'We've just had lunch. Is your arthritis worse then?'

'I'm afraid it is, my dear. It's getting harder to get around. But I get plenty of help, you know. I have a woman who comes in every morning to do the housework and shopping.'

'That's good,' said Emily.

'And are you better, Emily? Everyone was so worried about you last term.'

'Yes, I'm fine now, thanks,' Emily replied with a big smile.

'You certainly look bonnie enough. Give me a hand up, there's a dear. The wind is feeling a little chilly. Let's go inside.'

The girls followed Mrs Allingham into her cottage, which was crammed full of antiques and curios.

'Would you like to see my old costumes?' she asked them. 'My daughter's just returned them to me. She's about to move and hasn't room to store them in her new house.'

'Can I stay with the cats?' asked Becky. Tinker and Marmalade had trotted into the sitting-room and found the most comfortable cushions to lie on.

'Of course you may!'

The others followed the old lady into a small side

room where there was a full-length, recessed cupboard.

'I've had this converted into a wardrobe for the costumes,' she explained. Mrs Allingham opened the doors to reveal over twenty tutus and calf-length net dresses of various shades and styles.

The girls pounced on them, taking each one out in turn and holding it against themselves.

'Ooh, this one's gorgeous!' cried Cassie, picking out a shimmering lilac tutu.

'That was my Lilac Fairy costume,' said Mrs Allingham, smiling. 'It is pretty, isn't it?'

'Is that from *The Sleeping Beauty*?' asked Poppy.

'Yes, that's right,' said Mrs Allingham. 'She's the fairy who changes the bad fairy's curse.'

'How many times did you dance the role?' asked Cassie.

'Oh, just the one season, but I enjoyed it immensely. The next time we did *The Sleeping Beauty*, I danced Aurora, and that was quite something!'

'Was that your favourite role?' asked Cassie.

'I think it was, with the exception of Giselle.'

Cassie looked through the rack of costumes. 'Which is the Aurora costume?'

'This one,' said Mrs Allingham. 'The rose-pink tutu.'

'Oh, it's lovely!' cried Emily.

'It must be hard for you to imagine a poor old cripple like me prancing about in these dresses,' said Mrs Allingham, laughing. 'How are you getting on with your dancing, Emily, after the break you had?'

'I'm catching up, I think,' said Emily, 'but it'll be

21

hard getting back into shape. You get out of the habit of practising. My body really complained the first night. To be honest, I'm still pretty achy now.'

'Weren't you able to practise at all at home?'

'No, my doctor wouldn't let me.'

'How very frustrating for you.'

'I don't know. Looking back, I think he was right. I needed a rest from it. And my flute-playing improved no end!'

'The flute!' cried Mrs Allingham. 'Would you play my old flute for me? It hasn't had a tune played on it for years.'

Emily was only too happy to oblige, especially when she saw the lovely silver instrument that Mrs Allingham brought out of a drawer. She played a couple of short melodies on it. Cassie could see the delight in Mrs Allingham's eyes as she listened.

'Emily's becoming a bit of a star, isn't she?' Cassie remarked at the end of the second tune.

'Indeed, indeed,' said the old lady, looking as pleased as Punch. 'I used to love playing the flute before my hands seized up! Well done, Emily!'

The time had passed by so quickly that Cassie was amazed when she looked at her watch.

'We must dash,' she said.

They would only just make it back in time for afternoon school, if they ran all the way. But as they sprinted past the girls' wing, they bumped into the skinny workman. They came to a breathless halt. Cassie was pleased that the surveyor was nowhere in sight.

'There you are,' the workman said. 'I've bin asking a few questions for you,' he explained. 'You wanted to know what all the scaffolding was for?'

'Yes, that's right,' said Cassie eagerly. The others were starting to tug at her sleeve, conscious that the lesson bell would ring at any moment.

'Well, your wing's slipping away from the rest of the building.'

Cassie gasped. 'Slipping away!' she exclaimed.

'Yes,' said the workman. 'If something isn't done quick, the whole lot could collapse.'

3

Moving

A week later, the school assembly was informed by Miss Wrench that the girls' wing was subsiding.

'Old news to us,' Becky whispered to Cassie.

'Shsh,' said Cassie, seeing Miss Oakland cast a sharp glance in their direction.

'This is very unfortunate,' went on Miss Wrench, 'particularly since the building is now considered dangerous.'

Cassie and Becky looked at one another, shocked.

'All the girls at present housed in the wing are to be evacuated. The boys' block is to be reorganised today, to take in the girls.'

Cassie's eyes opened very wide. Becky blinked hard.

'I'm afraid it will mean being rather overcrowded for a while, but dancers must learn to cope with all manner of difficulties in accommodation, so this will be a good lesson for all of you.'

Miss Wrench's face looked stern and anxious as she finished the assembly and dismissed her pupils.

'No wonder she's been looking worried lately,' said Emily afterwards in the science lab.

'She must be scared to death putting us with the boys!' said Cassie. 'Oh, what am I supposed to be doing with this bunsen burner?'

Becky laughed at Cassie and showed her what to do. 'It's funny they haven't started doing repair work, if it's that urgent. I mean, since the scaffolding has all gone up, we haven't seen any more of the workmen, have we?'

'No, just that horrible little sandy-haired surveyor,' said Poppy. 'He's still nosing around.'

'I expect they've got to evacuate us first,' said Cassie. 'It'll be fun really, moving into the boys' block.'

'Perhaps we should wait and see what it's like,' suggested Emily, more cautiously.

They were told they would be moving the next day. The dining-hall at lunch-time was buzzing with the news. Cassie found Matthew, Ojo and Tom and asked them what had been going on in their block.

'We've been moved,' said Matthew glumly. 'We're sharing a room with three third years – six beds in a room designed for three.'

'It's not much fun,' said Tom. 'The third years throw

26

their weight around all the time.'

'Oh poor you,' said Cassie. She turned to Ojo. 'Any idea yet when you'll be back dancing again?'

He shrugged, looking dejected. 'The consultant still hasn't given me a date. Says it's not healing as well as it might.'

'Well, it's got to get better sometime,' said Cassie, trying to be cheerful.

'We'll be seeing a bit more of you from tomorrow then,' said Matthew, with an attempt at a smile.

'That's right,' said Cassie. She moved back to her friends.

'The boys are pretty miserable,' she reported.

'We'll cheer 'em up tomorrow!' said Becky. 'Come on, we must go. It's orchestra practice.'

'Drat, I'd forgotten. See you later, Emily.'

'I'm coming too,' said Emily with a smile.

'Have you joined then? You didn't let on,' said Cassie.

'Yes, Mrs Longville said I'd made such progress on my flute that I could sit in the front row of the flautists.'

'Oh, Emily, that's wonderful!' cried Cassie. 'I'm so pleased for you.'

Emily looked exceedingly pleased with herself when she took up her position in the orchestra, and the practice began. The students were to learn a programme of simplified orchestral favourites, which they would play in the end-of-term Gala.

'It'll be funny being on stage with a flute, instead of ballet shoes,' said Emily at the end of the rehearsal.

'Yes, it will make a change,' said Cassie. 'I hope I manage to learn the first violin parts well enough. That Mozart piece was hard, wasn't it?'

'Lovely, though. What did you think, Celia?' Emily asked the girl, who had just approached.

'I suppose you think you're an expert already, Emily Pickering,' said Celia with a toss of her head. 'And on your very first rehearsal too!'

Emily laughed. 'I know what I like, that's all!'

'Oh, I think there's a touch of green in your eye,' said Cassie to Celia.

'I'm not jealous of anyone,' scoffed Celia. 'Don't forget, I'm doing my Grade Six soon.'

'Grades aren't everything,' said Emily. 'It's the sound you make that matters in the end.'

'Are you trying to say my tone's useless?'

'No, of course not,' said Emily, but Celia, looking unconvinced, walked off in a huff.

'I don't think Celia is very happy about you going in at first desk,' said Cassie. 'She will never forgive you for getting on so fast.'

'Well, who cares?' said Emily. 'I don't.'

Nothing appeared to dent Emily's new-found happiness. Any worries Cassie had had at the beginning of term about Emily's anorexia or family problems reappearing had been allayed. Altogether, Emily seemed more well-balanced and contented than she'd ever been.

The next day began with high excitement when Miss Eiseldown told the girls they were excused academic lessons up to lunch-time in order to pack and move their belongings to their new accommodation.

'What about ballet class?' asked Becky, hopefully.

'No, you won't be missing that,' said Miss Eiseldown, with a wry smile. 'Just remember what sort of school you're in!'

'Oh, I've just thought,' moaned Becky, 'we'll be missing your maths lesson!'

'I'm flattered you're disappointed,' said Miss Eiseldown, 'though I don't see many other downcast faces.'

Their house-mother was right. Cassie, for one, was all too glad to escape Maths for once.

The feeling of excitement stayed with the girls until they arrived at Studio One for their class. They went in to the class chatting noisily, and Miss Oakland came down on them like a ton of bricks. Sheepishly, they took their places at the barre and began the rigorous training that was demanded of them.

Cassie's group, which included Abigail, Poppy, Emily and Celia, was working for the Elementary exam. There was far more pointe work in the syllabus and harder pirouettes. Cassie was enjoying learning the new steps and exercises immensely. She hoped this time she would do herself justice in the exam – maybe even gaining Honours. She hadn't prepared properly for her last major exam, and had been bitterly disappointed with the result.

At the end of class, the girls couldn't wait to get back to their rooms. They flung their clothes and belongings into trunks and suitcases, and sat on the lids to close them. But then, after that great flurry of activity, they had to sit and wait for their house-mother to send for them; the move to the boys' block was being conducted in an orderly fashion.

When the signal came, the girls in Cassie's room set off at a great pace. Cassie was surprised to find they were joined by Abigail, Celia, Jane and Yoko, the small Japanese girl, from another room.

'I thought they were moving us one room at a time,' she said.

'This is one room,' said Abigail, indicating all the girls trundling over with heavy suitcases.

Cassie stopped a moment to catch her breath.

'You, mean all *eight* of us, in one room?'

'That's what Miss Eiseldown told us,' said Abigail.

Cassie's heart sank. Sharing a room with Celia was not going to be fun.

When they arrived at the boys' block, which was separate and a little to one side of the main building, Mr Whistler met them at the entrance and showed them to Room 13 – their new room.

Cassie groaned when she saw the number. 'This doesn't sound too promising,' she said.

'You're not superstitious, are you?' laughed Mr Whistler, flicking his dark hair out of his eyes.

Cassie smiled at him. 'Only about some things,' she said.

He left them to unpack. Cassie looked at the cramped room and wondered how they would manage to get along without squabbles.

The eight beds took up most of the floor space.

There were no desks for homework, and very little storage space, though Mr Whistler was going to get a couple of chests of drawers from the girls' wing. Cassie missed the homely feel of her old room; this one was modern and very plain, with only a small window. Becky sighed and sat on her bed dreamily.

'What's up?' asked Cassie.

'Oh, I was just thinking how marvellous it's going to be living in the same block as Mr Whistler.'

Mr Whistler was house-father to the younger boys.

'What's so marvellous about that?' asked Celia scathingly.

'Didn't you know Becky has a crush on Mr Whistler?' said Abigail, trying to stop Celia from saying any more.

But Celia was unstoppable. 'I wish he'd get a haircut,' she said. 'It hangs like two curtains either side of his face.'

'Lovely!' breathed Becky.

Cassie was relieved that Celia wasn't getting to Becky at least.

'Miss Eiseldown said she'd got a very tiny room on our floor.'

'Yes, they've converted the broom cupboard!' said Poppy. 'I heard the boys talking about it yesterday.'

'So we're all on the ground floor, and the boys are upstairs. Is that right?' asked Emily.

'Yes,' said Poppy, 'except for some of the senior girls – they're upstairs too. There wasn't room for them down here.'

'Just think,' sighed Becky, 'one of their rooms might

be right next to Mr Whistler's!'

'Oh, how wonderful!' Celia mimicked.

There was a tap on the door. Cassie let in Mr Whistler and Matthew, who were carrying a chest of drawers between them. They managed to squeeze it in a corner and went off again to fetch another one.

When space was found for that the room seemed smaller than ever, but at least there were two drawers apiece now.

Miss Eiseldown popped in to see how they were getting on.

'It's hopeless!' cried Cassie. 'We've got all this equipment and nowhere to put it. It reminds me of when I've been camping with my family.'

'I think you will have to keep a lot of your stuff in your cases under your beds,' the house-mother suggested. 'You'll manage.'

'There won't be room for my cello, then,' said Becky.

'You can keep larger instruments in the main music room,' said Miss Eiseldown. 'And practising will have to be confined to the practice rooms. You'll get on one another's nerves otherwise.'

'What about my flute?' asked Emily. 'It doesn't take up a lot of space, and I'd like to be able to play it in here now and then.'

'You can certainly keep it in here,' said Miss Eiseldown, 'but if you want to play, you must ask your room-mates first.'

Cassie didn't like the look on Celia's face when Miss Eiseldown said this. She hoped she wouldn't try to stop Emily practising out of spite.

The day proceeded normally for the girls after lunch, except that they had to go to a classroom for their preparation period instead of back to their room. After rehearsals and supper, they made their way across the grounds to their new block.

'It's really funny going out of school to our room,' said Emily. 'I suppose we'll get used to it.'

'I'm glad it's spring,' said Cassie. 'The evenings are light and warm. It would be a different story in the winter.'

'Hey, do you think we might still be over here by then?' asked Poppy.

'I certainly hope not,' said Cassie. 'No, I'm sure they'll get on with the repairs quickly.'

'Will it be a big job, do you think?'

'I think they have to do something called underpinning. That's what Miss Eiseldown said, anyway, but I don't know how long it will take.'

They got back to their room just before Celia and Abigail. Yoko and Jane were already on their way to the bathroom with towels and night-clothes.

The rehearsal had been very energetic and they all wanted a refreshing shower, but Jane came back with bad news. 'There's a queue,' she said. 'There aren't enough showers to go round.'

Everyone groaned. 'We'd better get a place in the queue then,' said Cassie, picking up her towel and wash-bag.

All eight of the girls joined the queue, which had spilled out into the corridor.

'This really is just like camping,' said Cassie. She was beginning to see the funny side of it all.

Suddenly, there was a strange noise from the far end of the corridor. Cassie looked round Poppy's shoulder to see what it was.

Matthew and Tom were pelting towards them, whooping loudly. The girls had to flatten themselves against the wall to let them pass.

Cassie and Poppy looked at one another in surprise.

'Whatever are they up to?' asked Becky.

'I thought this floor was out of bounds to the boys!' raged Celia. She looked extremely cross.

'That wouldn't stop Matthew,' Cassie laughed.

'Well, I shall report them to Mr Whistler,' said Celia.

'No, don't do that,' said Abigail. 'They didn't do any harm really.'

'I don't want boys hanging round our quarters all the time,' Celia argued.

'Oh, give it a rest, Celia,' Cassie broke in.

When the girls eventually worked their way to the front of the queue, Celia was still muttering about the boys. 'You never know where they're going to pop up next!' she complained.

Abigail had stripped off, ready for her shower. 'Come on, Celia,' she said gently. 'Just forget about the boys.'

'We won't get any privacy,' muttered Celia, who had only taken off her outer clothes. She strode into the shower cubicle, still wearing her knickers and thermal vest.

'Celia,' cried Abigail, 'you've forgotten your—'

'I know, silly,' snapped Celia. 'I'm not taking any chances.'

The whole room erupted into laughter, and as the joke trickled back down the queue, a wave of laughter washed down the corridor.

Celia's face was fiery red when she came out of the shower.

'I'll get you back for this,' she spluttered. 'All of you!'

Abigail tried to calm her down, but with little success.

'Well if nothing else, we've had a laugh,' said Cassie to Becky. 'Perhaps life in the boys' block is going to be fun after all!'

4

Room 13

As the days went by, the girls got used to their new room. Everyone had to be extremely tidy and polite, as it was so easy to get on one another's nerves in such cramped conditions. Miss Eiseldown continued to inspect their room in the mornings, just as she had done in the girls' wing. She was so pleased with the way they were managing, she awarded them the gold star for the month – a great honour.

Of course, Celia took every opportunity to let the other students know that it was her influence which had won them the gold star. Cassie winced every time she heard her starting up the subject, but tried to hold her tongue. She didn't want a bad atmosphere in Room 13.

A couple of nights after they'd had their gold star, Celia got into bed and screamed.

'Whatever's the matter?' yelled Abigail.

But Celia couldn't speak. She shot up and sat on her pillow, knees tucked up under her chin, and jabbed her finger towards the mattress.

Abigail and Cassie cautiously pulled back the duvet on Celia's bed.

'Yuck!' said Cassie.

Crawling over the bottom sheet was a big black slimy slug.

'Do something!' Celia screeched, suddenly finding her voice. 'Which one of you has done this?'

Cassie looked at her in surprise. 'None of us would put a slug in your bed!'

'Well who did, then?' demanded Celia. 'Get it away from me!' she shrieked, as it began oozing its way towards her.

Becky calmly got out of bed, scooped up the offending creature and lowered it gently out of the window.

'It's a good job we've got you around,' said Cassie. 'I don't mind most creepy-crawlies, but slugs are the pits!'

The slug mystery was not solved until breakfast next day, when Matthew and Tom stopped the friends on their way to a table.

'Did Celia sleep well?' asked Matthew, with a cheeky grin.

Cassie quickly put two and two together. 'Oh, it was you lot, was it?' she said, hands on hips. 'Celia won't believe it wasn't one of us. You'd better own up.'

'No fear,' said Matthew. 'She'd report us straight away.'

'Well, I should leave her alone, if I were you,' said Cassie. 'It'll just make life more difficult for all of us if you don't.'

'But it was just a bit of fun,' said Matthew.

'We were sick of hearing about the gold star,' added Tom.

Celia refused to speak to anyone from Room 13 except Abigail, for the rest of the day. As they all changed into their practice clothes in the late afternoon, ready for rehearsals for the Gala, Cassie tried to strike up a conversation with her.

'Look, Celia, I know you had a nasty shock, but it really wasn't any of us.'

No answer.

'Believe me, Celia. We knew nothing about it.'

No answer.

'Come on, Celia. This is silly. We've all got to get along together in this cramped room.'

'Perhaps she'd believe you if you found out who *had* put the slug in her bed,' suggested Abigail.

Cassie sighed. She wanted to clear the air, but giving away Matthew and Tom wouldn't be fair.

The rehearsal did not include *Cinderella*, for a change. Madame had choreographed a short new ballet to Pachelbel's beautiful *Canon*. The girls would all wear classical white, calf-length ballet dresses. The boys would wear black tights and romantic white shirts. Madame had yet to audition for the boys' parts, and so all the boys went off to the other studio with their ballet master, to rehearse another item.

The 'Canon Ballet', as it came to be known, was rather like *Les Sylphides*, with the dancers forming graceful and intricate patterns. There would be no soloists among the girls; the emphasis was on working as a group, harmoniously and gracefully.

Cassie was full of admiration for Madame's choreography. But the ballet mistress lacked her usual enthusiasm, as she marked out the sequences with them. She almost seemed half-hearted in her teaching.

'Non, non, not like that,' she cried out at one point in the rehearsal, when some of the girls, including Cassie, had misunderstood her instructions.

'You really must *listen*!' she said impatiently. 'Let's do it again. And one . . .'

'Whatever was wrong with Madame?' cried Cassie, as they emerged into the changing-room.

'Goodness knows,' said Becky. 'One of her migraines starting up, maybe.'

'I don't know, Becky. Everything seems strange at school at the moment.'

'It's not that bad, is it?'

'And I'll tell you something else. You'd think they'd be wanting to repair our wing really quickly, wouldn't you?'

'Yes,' Becky agreed, puzzled.

'Well, I haven't seen a single workman since we moved, have you?'

'Well no,' Becky had to admit. 'I hadn't thought about it, but it does seem funny.'

When they got back to their room after supper, Jane looked upset. As Celia hadn't yet returned with Abigail, Cassie felt able to talk to her more openly.

'What is it, Jane? Celia hasn't been getting at you again, has she?'

'No, no,' said Jane. 'She's not speaking to me.'

'What is it then?'

'It's the rehearsals,' Jane blurted out. 'They keep reminding me that I won't be returning after the Gala. And my parents have refused to come and watch now that I've got to leave. They're so cross with Miss Wrench.'

Cassie could sympathise with Jane's anguish. 'I'm really sorry you've got to leave, Jane,' she said. 'But you might get into another good school, don't forget that! And your parents will come round before the Gala, I'm sure.'

They broke off their conversation as Abigail and Celia walked in. Celia looked at them suspiciously.

'S'pose you're cooking up another silly trick to play on me!' she said suddenly.

'Well, I'm glad you're speaking to us again,' said Cassie, 'but no, we're not doing anything of the sort.'

'You can't fool me,' Celia snorted. 'I can tell by the look on your faces that you were planning something when we came in.'

'No Celia, that's not true!' Jane burst out.

41

'Well, you've got nothing to lose have you, Miss Plain Jane?' Celia blundered on. 'They can't really expel you, when you've already had the shove!'

Cassie couldn't take any more. A hot feeling of anger welled up inside her and burst out.

'I told you to leave Jane alone!' she said. Her voice stayed quiet, but Abigail recognized a dangerous quality in it.

'Come on Celia, leave it,' said Abigail. But Celia was far too thick-skinned to stop now.

'I'll do what I like, Cassandra Brown!' she yelled.

'No, you won't!' shouted Cassie, her voice rising with her temper. 'While we're all sharing a room, you'd better try hard to get along with everyone. Otherwise you might find yourself with six or seven girls not speaking to you!'

Her speech over, Cassie felt much calmer, but she could see that Celia was still furious. It was time to get out of her way.

'Come with me to Mrs Allingham's,' she whispered to Becky and, before Celia could start shouting again, they had left the room.

'We're not supposed to go out after supper,' Becky reminded her outside.

'We'll be careful,' said Cassie. 'I just had to get away from Celia.'

'It'll give Mrs Allingham a nice surprise,' said Becky, as they walked across the lawns towards the cottage.

'Yes,' agreed Cassie. 'I don't suppose she often has visitors in the evening.'

When they reached the rose-framed front door, all seemed quiet.

They knocked and waited, but no one came. Cassie shouted through the letter-box but only Tinker appeared. He came round to the front, miaowing and rubbing his head against Becky's ankles. It wasn't long before Marmalade joined him, also miaowing loudly.

'They seem hungry,' said Becky, 'and Mrs Allingham must have gone out for the evening. I wonder if she'd mind if we went in to feed them? Do you remember where she hides her spare back door key?'

'Yes, in the pansy tub,' said Cassie. 'I should think it would be OK. She must have forgotten about the cats, although it isn't like her.'

The girls went through the little wooden gate at the side of the house, and walked round to the back, to fetch the key.

'Do you think she often goes out in the evenings?' asked Becky.

'I wouldn't have thought so,' said Cassie, as they let themselves into the back hallway. 'We ought to give her a shout, in case she is here. She might think she's got burglars otherwise.' The girls called Mrs Allingham's name, but there was no reply.

'Now where does she keep the cat food?' said Becky, hunting through the kitchen cupboards.

Tinker seemed to know what Becky was looking for. He parked himself next to the cupboard under the sink and went through chewing motions with his mouth.

Cassie and Becky laughed at him.

'He really is a very clever cat,' said Becky, proudly.

'It must have been living with us when he was tiny,' said Cassie, stroking his black coat, while Becky opened a tin of cat food and shared it out between two dishes.

'That's funny,' said Cassie, who had wandered into the dining-room. 'Mrs Allingham's supper is sitting here on the table untouched!'

'That's odd,' said Becky. 'Is it still warm?'

'No, it's gone cold!'

Cassie began to have an uncomfortable feeling that something was amiss. 'We'd better have a look round, I think,' she said.

The girls looked in the sitting-room. Empty. 'What about upstairs?' Becky suggested.

The two girls looked at each other. 'Mrs Allingham!' Cassie called from the hall. Her voice sounded hollow. 'Mrs Allingham!'

A sense of foreboding washed over the two friends. The stairs stretched up in front of them. Cassie gulped.

'You don't think something's happened to her?' Becky whispered in Cassie's ear, as they started up the stairs.

'Shh! Listen!' Cassie hissed. They could hear a pained moaning sound.

Cassie braced herself and continued silently up the stairs, followed by Becky. They were both trembling.

When they reached the landing, Cassie let out a shriek. 'Oh no! Look Becky!'

Mrs Allingham was lying on the floor of the bathroom. She was making the gurgling, moaning sound they had heard on the stairs. She was obviously trying to speak to them, but couldn't.

'Mrs Allingham!' cried Cassie, running across to kneel down beside her. 'What's happened?'

'Don't move her,' Becky warned. 'She might have fallen and broken something.'

'But why can't she speak?' wailed Cassie, fighting back her tears.

'I don't know,' said Becky, looking terribly worried, 'but she needs medical attention. You look after her, while I go and ring for an ambulance.'

Becky rushed off downstairs and Cassie stroked Mrs Allingham's grey hair, soothing her as best she could. She began talking to her gently. Mrs Allingham obviously understood everything Cassie said to her, but her inability to reply distressed her.

'Don't try to answer. I'll speak for both of us,' Cassie whispered.

During the long ten minutes that it took the ambulance to arrive, Cassie never stopped talking to her elderly friend. She told her all about the Easter tour, and the dances they were going to do in the end-of-year Gala. She talked about their move to the boys' block and the scaffolding round the girls' wing. In fact everything on her mind came tumbling out, and Cassie's comforting chatter seemed to take Mrs Allingham's mind off her distress.

Meanwhile, Becky packed a couple of nightdresses and a toiletries bag for Mrs Allingham to take to the hospital. Her mind in a whirl, she hoped she'd remembered all the important things.

At last the ambulance arrived, and Becky showed the ambulancemen upstairs. Mrs Allingham was carefully lifted on to a stretcher and carried downstairs. The girls followed her down to the garden. The old lady suddenly reached out with her left hand towards her pets who were waiting by the gate. The girls lifted them up for her to stroke.

'Don't worry about Tinker and Marmers,' said Becky. 'We'll come across every day and feed them, won't we, Cassie?'

'Of course we will. Just get better soon – they'll miss you, like we shall.'

Mrs Allingham gave a weak lopsided smile, then she was lifted into the ambulance. The doors were shut and the ambulance drove off.

When Cassie and Becky went back into the cottage, it felt uncomfortably empty. It was hard to believe they had just watched Mrs Allingham go off to hospital and yet the silence in the cottage convinced them it was so. They did a bit of half-hearted tidying up, locked the door after them and set off back to school.

Cassie felt a great lump in her throat which prevented her from speaking for some time. Becky also walked in silence, her eyes to the ground,

'It's not fair,' said Cassie at last. 'She's such a dear old lady. She shouldn't have to be ill!'

'No,' Becky agreed. 'It was such a shock finding her like that!'

'It's a good job we did find her,' said Cassie. She shuddered. 'It would have been horrible for her to spend the rest of the night on the floor.'

'She seemed to be paralysed down one side, poor thing,' said Becky.

'I suppose we'd better let Miss Wrench know, so she can phone Mrs Allingham's daughter,' said Cassie.

'But then we'll have to admit we were breaking school rules,' Becky protested.

'I know,' said Cassie, 'but we've got to do it.'

They walked off in the direction of the main school.

'I wonder if she'll be in her study at this time, or in her bedroom?' asked Becky.

'Let's try the study first,' Cassie suggested.

When they got there, and knocked on the door, Miss Wrench's voice called to them to wait outside.

They sat in the small lobby, and could now detect a man's voice in conversation with the Principal.

When he emerged, they were surprised to find it was Mr Smithson, the sandy-haired surveyor. He had an unpleasantly smug smile on his face as he came out, which he wiped off the instant he saw the girls.

'Come in, now,' said Miss Wrench.

The girls went in. Miss Wrench looked very pale and Cassie noticed that her hands were trembling.

'What is it girls? I hope it's something important, disturbing me at this hour!'

'Yes, it is important, Miss Wrench,' said Cassie, dropping a curtsey. 'We've just seen Mrs Allingham off in an ambulance.'

Miss Wrench sat down heavily. 'Oh no. What's the matter with her, Cassandra?'

'We found her in the bathroom. She'd fallen and couldn't get up, and she couldn't speak to us!' Cassie's voice started to break.

'I think her right side was paralysed,' added Becky.

'Oh, how awful! That sounds like a stroke,' cried Miss Wrench. 'Poor June! How fortunate you found her. Leave it to me – I'll make sure the right people are notified.'

She stood up and walked with them to the door. Her hand still trembled as she reached for the doorknob.

'Thank you girls. Good evening.'

She seemed eager to get rid of them.

'I can't believe she didn't tell us off for going out after supper!' cried Becky, when they were out of earshot of the study.

'It's almost as though she didn't think of it,' said Cassie. 'That's not like Miss Wrench at all.'

'She looked upset, didn't she?' said Becky. 'I mean, even before we told her the news about Mrs Allingham.'

'I thought so too,' agreed Cassie. 'It must have had something to do with the visit from Mr Smithson. I really don't like that man!'

'I'm not looking forward to telling Emily and Poppy about Mrs A.,' said Becky.

'No,' said Cassie. 'I wonder how long she'll be in hospital? We'll have to visit her, to keep her cheerful.

Her family live such a long way away, I don't suppose she'll see much of them.'

'We could write to her, too – keep her up-to-date with all the gossip,' said Becky. 'We'll have her better in no time,' she added, trying to sound confident.

Cassie tried to push to the back of her mind the expression of pain on the old lady's face when they found her, and how frail she'd looked on the stretcher. Now she and Becky just wanted to look ahead to their friend's recovery, to a time when they would once again be sipping lemonade in Mrs Allingham's Aladdin's cave of a cottage.

5

Shockwaves

There was an announcement at breakfast next morning. Miss Waters, who happened to be on duty, told them that there would be a special assembly immediately after break, for the whole school.

'Oh no,' groaned Poppy. 'They're always a terrible crush.'

Cassie turned to Becky. 'I bet this has something to do with Mr Smithson's meeting with Miss Wrench last night.'

'Not more bad news, surely?' said Becky. The friends were still upset about Mrs Allingham's sudden illness.

'Everything's starting to go wrong,' said Emily, 'just when things were so much better for me.'

'Well, there's no point worrying yet,' said Cassie. 'Let's wait and see what the Wrench has to say.'

When everyone had been packed into the assembly hall, Miss Wrench mounted the platform looking grim-faced. There were to be no hymns or prayers this morning. She asked them all to sit down. For the Juniors, this meant sitting cross-legged on the hard oak floor. She omitted her usual greeting and began addressing the school in a sombre voice.

'Today is a sad day for Redwood. The structures of the main building, along with the girls' wing, have been officially classed as dangerous. Subsidence is so substantial that it would take a quarter of a million pounds to put it right.' She paused, struggling to keep her voice under control. 'A quarter of a million pounds that the school does not have.'

Cassie had steeled herself for bad news, but this sounded ominous. She, along with all the other students, listened intently to their Principal's next words. There was not a sound in the hall except Miss Wrench's flat, tired-sounding voice.

'The girls' wing has already been evacuated, but we can only go on using the main building for a matter of weeks. After that, Redwood Ballet School must close. I'm sorry to have to break such awful news to you. I shall be writing to each of your parents this morning and the staff will be available to give you advice and support about alternative places in other establishments.'

The students were always silent in assembly, but after Miss Wrench had left the platform, the silence became intense; the sense of shock was palpable. As Handel's Water Music came over the speakers, a signal for them to file out, they stood dumbfounded. Music after assembly was a tradition, usually comforting and safe. But now it struck all of them that everything familiar was set to change. They went about the tasks of the morning in a trance-like state. But by lunch-time, tongues were loosened.

'I just can't believe it!' said Cassie, pushing the food round her plate. No one seemed to have an appetite.

'It's so much worse for you,' said Becky. 'I mean, I never wanted to be a dancer anyway.'

'I can't imagine going to another ballet school,' said Cassie, 'and I'm not sure my parents could afford to send me anywhere else. The scholarship here made all the difference.'

'Same here,' said Emily, glumly.

'I'll have to go back to Australia,' said Poppy. 'At least I know I have a place at my old dancing academy, but I'll miss all of you terribly.'

'Oh don't,' said Cassie. 'I hate thinking of us all splitting up, going our separate ways.'

'No wonder the Wrench looked upset last night!' said Becky. 'Mr Smithson must have just told her the bad news when we arrived.'

'The staff must have suspected it for a while,' said Cassie. 'That would explain the strange atmosphere in the school.'

'And to think it all started with a few cracks in our buildings in the holidays!' cried Poppy. 'It happened so quickly!'

'You don't think we'll close before the end of term, do you?' Emily asked anxiously.

Cassie looked into her troubled eyes. The Gala! It would be a terrible blow to Emily if she never had her chance to dance Cinderella.

'I don't know, Em,' she answered truthfully. 'Let's ask Madame at the rehearsal.' But Cassie didn't need to ask the ballet mistress. The sadness in her face said it all, when they walked into the rehearsal room after preparation.

'I'm sorry, girls and boys,' she said gently, when all the students had come into the studio, 'but the school may have to close by half-term. So our plans for the Gala 'ave to be given up.'

There were sighs of disappointment all round her.

'I'm sorry,' she said again. 'We must all be miserable together.'

Trying to keep everyone's spirits up, she gave a pas de deux lesson instead of the planned rehearsal.

Cassie was partnered by Matthew. As they worked on balancing poses together, Cassie could see he was as unhappy as any of her other friends.

'What will you do?' she whispered.

'It's just the chance my stepfather's been waiting for,' said Matthew. 'He wants me to follow some sensible career like banking!'

'It's going to mean the end of dancing hopes for many of us,' sighed Cassie.

Later, in the changing-rooms, Emily burst into tears. 'I can't bear the thought of the school closing,' she sobbed. 'And I did so want to be Cinderella.'

'I know,' said Cassie, putting a comforting arm round her. 'It's really hard to accept.'

Jane came over to them. 'Something will turn up for you, you know.'

'Any idea where you're going yet?' asked Cassie.

'I've got an audition for Longford School next week. Cross your fingers for me.'

'Oh, Jane, I'm thrilled for you. Perhaps things will work out better for you than the rest of us!'

Celia couldn't resist poking her nose in.

'Typical!' she said. 'The worst of us will take all the good places before the best of us have a chance to apply!'

The girls were reminded after supper of their other anxiety. Miss Wrench had given them permission to go across to Mrs Allingham's cottage every evening to feed the cats. The home-help was able to give them their breakfast.

Poppy decided to go with Cassie and Becky, but Emily was too upset.

'I don't want to see the cottage all lonely without her,' she said. 'It'll make me feel worse. I'll stay here and play my flute instead. At least I still have that.'

'No you won't,' Celia cut in. She was reading on her bed. 'It'll put me off my book.'

'Don't be so selfish,' said Cassie crossly. 'You can see Emily's upset. It'll cheer her up to play her flute.'

'Selfish!' cried Celia. 'I like that! Emily can go to a practice room. I was here first.'

Cassie opened her mouth to argue, but Emily frowned at her. 'It's all right,' she said. 'Perhaps I ought to come across with you after all. I can play as we walk.'

The haunting melody of Emily's flute, as they walked across the empty, peaceful grounds conjured up feelings of sadness they all shared.

Tinker and Marmalade were delighted to see them, when they reached the cottage.

'They must be lonely,' said Becky, picking up Tinker for a cuddle. 'I hope Mrs Allingham doesn't have to stay in hospital for too long.'

'I'm going to ask Miss Eiseldown if we can visit her,' said Cassie.

Miss Eiseldown agreed to take the four girls to the Birmingham hospital the next evening.

'We'd better not tell Mrs A. the news about Redwood,' said Cassie, on the way to the hospital.

'No,' agreed Becky, 'we shouldn't worry her while she's ill.'

Miss Eiseldown drove them across the city to the hospital, after popping into a florists to buy some flowers.

'Ooh, this reminds me of being ill,' said Emily, as they walked to Mrs Allingham's ward. She shuddered. 'I've gone off hospitals.'

Mrs Allingham was overjoyed to see them. Although still very weak, she had a twinkle in her eye, and was delighted to hear about the cats.

The girls were relieved to find that Mrs Allingham had regained her power of speech, though it was a little indistinct. Cassie had to listen very carefully in order to understand what she said.

When Miss Eiseldown asked if there was anything she wanted, the old lady mumbled, 'A quarter of a million!'

Miss Eiseldown looked surprised.

'Have you heard about school then?' Cassie asked.

'Yes,' said Mrs Allingham. 'Miss Wrench came to see me yesterday.'

Cassie marvelled how the Principal had found time to visit her old friend on that day of all days.

'Cassandra,' whispered Mrs Allingham. 'You're a fighter, I know. A girl after my own heart! You mustn't give up hope. Fight, Cassandra, fight!'

Miss Eiseldown looked troubled, as they made their way back down the corridor. She stopped Cassie just as they reached the foyer.

'Don't take too much notice of what she said to you. She's not herself – probably drugged. I don't want you to feel, well, *responsible* for anything at school. I mean, it's out of all our hands, really. We did hope, for a while, that the repairs wouldn't be so extensive, and that the trust would afford them. But now . . .' She broke off and shrugged.

'What you youngsters must do is look to your futures. But outside Redwood!'

Miss Oakland advised the girls to work hard for their exams, the next morning in ballet class.

'I don't want to see you all slacking and moping about,' she said. 'We've got work to do. Many of you will want to continue your ballet training, so it makes sense to do your best in the forthcoming exam. Fortunately, we'll be able to fit it in before half-term. The dates have just come through this morning!'

Although it was hard, Cassie could see this was good advice, and settling down to work took her mind off all the troubles.

'Grands battements en cloche!' called Miss Oakland. 'And what does *cloche* mean, Poppy?'

'A bell, Miss Oakland,' Poppy answered.

'That's right. A smooth, continuous movement from fourth ouverte devant to fourth ouverte derrière. And one and . . .'

Cassie felt her thigh muscles being stretched, but she enjoyed the swinging, rhythmic movement of the exercise.

During their pointe work at the barre, Miss Oakland seemed particularly finickety, so Cassie tried her hardest to make her placing neat. Pointe work was always her favourite section, so she had little difficulty in turning out her best work.

During rises en pointe, Miss Oakland encouraged the girls to think of themselves as hot-air balloons – all uplift and lightness. With that in mind, they practised the more difficult temps de cou de pied; both feet snatched up together, one covering the other.

'No, no!' cried Miss Oakland in exasperation. 'You are landing like elephants. How can you prevent this . . . Cassandra?'

'By using the muscles in your instep, Miss Oakland.'

'Correct. But also, by controlling your breathing.

Inhale when you go up, but do not breathe out until you have landed. Remember this, please.'

Cassie found this little trick worked wonders. Suddenly her landings were much softer and smoother, her movements more controlled. All thoughts were suspended as she focused on her dancing. Cassie was doing what she loved most, and she didn't want the class to end. Afterwards, her spirits sank once more as the plight of her ballet school flooded back into her thoughts. Yoko looked equally miserable in the changing-room.

'My parents phoned this morning,' she sobbed. 'They think it too dangerous. I go back to Japan!'

As if this wasn't enough, Cassie bumped into Ojo and Matthew coming out of the changing-rooms. Ojo was still not joining in the classes and looked thoroughly dejected.

'Will you come to my party?' he asked Cassie.

'I'm not sure I'm in the mood,' Cassie answered. 'Is it your birthday or something?'

'No, it's my leaving party,' said Ojo with a wry smile. 'I'm going at the end of the week.'

'Why?' asked Cassie, in surprise.

'I spoke to my parents on the phone last night and they want me to transfer to my local school at home. I think it's best. It's been so boring the last few weeks, and since the school is closing down anyway, there's not much point in staying.'

'I see,' said Cassie. 'Does that mean you'll give up dancing?'

'Probably,' said Ojo. 'I don't care as much as I used

to. But you must all come to my party. Friday night in our room.'

'Can you share it with Yoko?' asked Cassie. 'She's leaving too this weekend. Her parents have got the jitters about her staying here. I suppose it must be worse for them being so far away. If anything did happen . . .' Her voice trailed off. Cassie knew her own parents would have their letter from Miss Wrench by now. She phoned them after supper. Her mum was very sympathetic, but when she asked her if she'd be able to go to another ballet school, Joy Brown put her husband on the phone.

'Can I, Dad?' she asked.

'I doubt it, love,' he said, and Cassie knew it hurt him to have to say it. 'The fees cost a fortune. There are the other kids to think of too.'

'What can I do then?' she said, a note of despair in her voice.

'We'll ask Madame for advice, but if the worst comes to the worst, you can always get tuition at home again.'

It would mean the end of her ambitions to be a professional dancer, and Cassie knew it, but she didn't want to make her dad feel even more guilty.

'Cassie, why don't you start an action committee? You know, like we did to save the village school?' Jake Brown suggested.

'A quarter of a million's a lot of money to raise,' said Cassie.

'Well, even if you could raise enough to pay for some shoring-up, it might at least allow the school to stay open till the end of term.'

60

'Thanks, Dad. It might be worth a try.'

Cassie put the phone down and thought about her father's suggestion. Mrs Allingham's words came back to her: 'Fight, Cassandra, fight.'

It was the only thing to do.

6

The Farewell Party

No one felt much like going to a party on Friday evening, but everyone agreed that Ojo and Yoko should be sent off from Redwood in a lively fashion.

The boys, who were sharing quite a large dormitory upstairs with some third years, did all the preparations themselves. Cassie was surprised that she and her friends hadn't been called on to help.

Cassie and her room-mates were the first girls to arrive. There were already several second year boys in the room. Lively music blared from Tom's cassette-player. All the beds had been pushed together to make more space, and the room had been decorated with balloons and streamers. Bowls of peanuts, crisps and chocolate biscuits had been placed on every surface.

'Let's start the dancing,' Ojo said to Yoko.

Yoko smiled shyly. 'But your leg!'

'I can keep my leg still and jiggle the rest of me about,' laughed Ojo.

'How did you manage to get rid of the third year boys?' Cassie asked Tom and Matthew.

'With difficulty,' said Matthew.

'We had to bribe them!' said Tom, wrinkling his nose in disgust.

'It's worth it, though,' said Matthew, 'just not to have them in the room for once.'

'Yes,' agreed Tom. 'They boss us around all the time!'

As more second years squeezed into the room, the dancing livened up. It was a chance to let themselves go, to move in ways that weren't choreographed for them with exacting precision. It was also a chance to forget the imminent closure of their school, at least for a short time.

Later, they filled their plastic cups with coke and toasted the leavers. Ojo said a few words of thanks and farewell. Yoko was too shy and uncertain of her English to speak to the whole group, so she asked Cassie to speak for her. Cassie was glad of the opportunity to air her thoughts to the assembled students.

'On behalf of Yoko, thank you for this send-off party. It's been great. Really, when you think about it, it is a farewell party for *all* of us. That is, unless we do something about it.'

'Like what?' shouted Celia.

'I want to form an action group to campaign against the closure of Redwood – or at least, to delay its closure.'

Squabbles immediately arose round the room between those who agreed with Cassie and those who thought it a waste of time and effort.

'If anyone thinks it's a good idea,' cried Cassie, above the noise, 'let's have a meeting to discuss it tomorrow afternoon in my room – Room 13 – at two o'clock. And spread the word. We need representatives from all years in the school!'

A sudden surge of optimism sprang up in the room, and there was a new frenzy of dancing. Cassie had hit upon a discovery: it was far better to do *something* than to give up hope and do nothing, even if the odds seemed stacked against you.

No one noticed how late it was getting, until the third year boys burst into the room.

'You lot still here!' said one of them, who was called Rob. He smiled nastily. 'We'll have to see what Whistling Willie has to say about this.'

He gestured to his friends to fetch the house-father, while he barred the door so that the girls couldn't get past.

'Come on,' argued Matthew. 'The party's finished now. Just let everyone go and you can get to bed. No problem.'

'But you're forgetting something,' Rob cut in. 'Second year bedtime is half-past eight.' He looked at his watch pointedly. 'Naughty. Naughty!'

'This is silly!' cried Cassie. 'Just let us go!'

She was just considering whether to try and barge past him, when Mr Whistler arrived. He was rather astonished to find so many girls in the room.

'Whatever's been going on?' he asked.

Matthew explained about the farewell party.

'Well, it's awfully late,' said Mr Whistler. 'But I won't report this, as it's a one-off.' Cassie could see Rob scowling out of the corner of her eye. 'But you girls better creep downstairs without a sound, or I'll have Miss Eiseldown after me!'

The thought of petite Miss Eiseldown going after the six-foot Mr Whistler was hilarious. But the girls did as they were told and, after saying goodbye to Ojo, who was going early the next morning, managed to get back to their room unnoticed.

'We got off lightly there,' said Becky, 'thanks to darling Mr Whistler!'

'I must say Cassie, I like your idea of an action group,' said Poppy, as they got into bed. 'I've thought of a few fund-raising activities already.'

'Save them till the meeting tomorrow,' said Cassie with a yawn. 'I'm shattered!'

They all overslept in the morning and had to be fished out of bed by Miss Eiseldown.

'You all look like zombies!' she said. 'I hope it's not getting you down too much, all this business about the school closing.'

'We're trying to be positive,' said Cassie. 'I'm going to hold a meeting this afternoon and hopefully we'll get an action group together then.'

66

'That's very enterprising of you, Cassandra,' said Miss Eiseldown. 'What sort of action were you thinking of instigating?'

'Well, fund-raising, mainly. We may not be able to stop the school closing, but maybe we could pay for enough repairs to keep it open till the end of term.'

'Yes, it's a good idea,' said the house-mother. 'Let me know how you get on. Is there anything I can do to help?'

'Well, yes, there is. Could you let the Seniors in your maths class this morning know about it?'

'Certainly,' said Miss Eiseldown. 'Good luck!'

The turn-out for the meeting was disappointing, even though the friends had scurried round the school through their break-time, pinning up hastily-made posters on every notice-board.

At two o'clock precisely, Cassie, Becky, Poppy and Emily sat in their room with the door open, waiting for people to arrive. At five past, Rhiannon and Abigail came in and sat down.

'Celia won't join,' said Abigail.

Cassie thanked her lucky stars. At ten past two, the girls had just decided to start the meeting, when three Seniors walked in. They were all fourth year pupils: Marianne, Jeanette and Lisa. The second years were a little in awe of these mature-looking young women, and Cassie suddenly felt her mouth go dry. Nevertheless, she managed to explain to them the aims of the action group and very soon plans were being drawn up for fund-raising activities.

Poppy suggested making badges. 'We could sell

them on Saturday afternoons in the village. Perhaps we might even get permission to take some into the city centre.'

'Do you mean have a caption like "Save Redwood"?' asked Rhiannon.

'Yes, that sort of thing,' agreed Poppy.

Then Cassie put forward her own brainchild.

'I thought we should present our own Gala,' she said. 'If we could get one ready for early June, say, we'd be able to mount it, even if Redwood closes before the end of term.'

Everyone agreed this was an inspired idea and Marianne offered to direct it.

'I've had a little experience at school of producing a ballet, just within our year group though,' she explained.

'That's fantastic,' said Cassie. 'And I'm sure we'll get a lot of volunteers of all ages to dance in it. I'd still like to do the excerpts from *Cinderella*.'

Emily's face lit up. 'Oh, that would be wonderful!' she said.

'A group of us fourth years have been working on a short contemporary piece,' said Lisa. 'Would you like that in the programme?'

'Oh yes,' said Cassie enthusiastically. 'It would make a great contrast. And I expect other years will have some other suggestions.'

'We mustn't forget about the other fund-raising projects, though,' said Becky, seeing everyone getting carried away with the Gala.

'No, you're right,' said Cassie, 'or we might not get

as far as the Gala. What's more important than anything is to get *everyone* involved, and everyone positive about saving Redwood!'

When the fourth years had gone, Cassie turned to Becky with a wistful look. 'Do you know what I wish?'

'No?'

'That Mrs Allingham will be well enough to come and see our Gala, like she always does.'

'Are you going to tell her about it?' Emily asked. The friends were going to visit her later that afternoon.

'Of course,' said Cassie. 'Just the thing to keep her cheerful. It was Mrs Allingham who gave me the idea of doing something in the first place.'

'She'll want her regular report on the cats,' said Becky. 'I thought I'd go and play with them before we go to the hospital.'

'I'll come with you,' said Cassie.

'I must do some flute practice,' said Emily. 'I seem to do more of that than ballet practice these days!'

The following week went by in a flurry of badge-making, rehearsing and spreading the news about the action group. Madame gave them permission to use Studio One to rehearse for their Gala, and gave them her blessing.

Yoko was given a tearful farewell at the beginning of the week and Jane went down to London with her mother on the Friday for her audition at the Longford Ballet School.

The friends expected her back at about seven, and

waited for her in Room 13 after supper.

'Let's hope our luck has changed,' said Cassie. 'Ever since we've been in this room, things have been going wrong.'

As soon as Jane opened the door, they knew she'd been accepted.

'They told me then and there,' she said, a huge smile of relief on her face.

Cassie was glad that Celia wasn't there to spoil Jane's moment of glory.

'Oh, well done!' she cried, giving her a big hug.

After being congratulated by everyone, Jane told them she'd liked the new school. It was smaller and less high-powered, but she'd felt at home there from the start.

'I just wish I could take you all with me!' she exclaimed.

Cassie was trying hard not to think of the future. Only her fund-raising plans were allowed into her consciousness. Beyond that was a blank that she did not dare fill. She continued to work very hard for her exam, which was less than a month away. She found all the work she was doing an excellent antidote to unhappy thoughts.

By Saturday, the action group had accumulated enough home-made badges to take into the village for sale. They each had the caption 'S.O.S. REDWOOD'. The friends had also made a billboard, explaining that their fund-raising was to save Redwood from closure.

The group of students attracted quite a lot of

interest from passing shoppers, who asked lots of questions as they bought their badges.

The weather was warm for early May, which made the whole exercise very pleasant. Cassie was just pinning a badge on the coat of an elderly gentleman, when out of the corner of her eye she saw a familiar face. She nudged Becky.

'Look, there's that surveyor fellow!'

Mr Smithson was talking on the opposite pavement to a taller man with a droopy moustache, who, after a couple of minutes, got into a new Mercedes parked nearby and drove off. The sandy-haired surveyor crossed the road and passed the girls.

'Hello,' Cassie called to him. 'Would you like a badge?'

Though so close, he hadn't seen them. Then he seemed to come out of his thoughts and consider what Cassie was holding up in front of him. His face twisted when he read the caption on the badge.

'No,' he said abruptly, 'you shouldn't go bothering people with those!'

'Typical!' cried Cassie, when he'd walked off. 'Wouldn't have hurt him to buy one!'

'Some people are just plain mean,' said Poppy, looking after him in disgust.

'I wonder who that man was he was talking to?' mused Cassie. 'He looked pretty well-off, didn't he?'

'Don't know,' said Emily. 'But look, Cassie, we've sold all the badges except three!'

Making over forty pounds was a good start to their

fund-raising and Cassie was delighted with the result. She wasn't so delighted when Miss Wrench saw her the next day.

'I've had a complaint,' said the Principal, having called Cassie into her study. 'One of our trustees saw you selling badges yesterday in the village. Mr Blane wanted to know what was going on. What is this all about Cassandra?'

Cassie explained as briefly as she could (which wasn't very) about their campaign.

'This is very enterprising of you all,' said Miss Wrench with a sigh, 'but we must face facts. The school is going to close down because we haven't got a quarter of a million pounds to stop it *falling* down.'

'I understand that, Miss Wrench,' said Cassie, 'but it's so much more positive to have something to work towards, than to give up and sit around moping.'

'You have your exam work,' Miss Wrench reminded her. 'For now that should be sufficient.'

'But maybe we could raise enough to keep the school open till the end of term?' said Cassie.

'That's unrealistic,' said Miss Wrench. 'And really, I must forbid any more fund-raising activities after this complaint from Mr Blane.'

'But, Miss Wrench!' burst out Cassie. 'We've started rehearsing a Gala of our own!'

'So I heard from Madame,' said the Principal. 'When is it likely to be ready?'

'We're aiming for the end of this half-term,' said Cassie eagerly.

'Mmm. What about your examination, Cassandra?'

72

Cassie blushed, remembering her previous poor effort. 'I won't make that mistake again,' she said. 'I'll work really hard, I promise.'

She could see Miss Wrench wavering. 'And it would be a lovely way to end; a really splendid Gala for the parents to come to!'

'Have you many pupils involved?'

'Yes, about thirty,' said Cassie. 'From first years to fourth years.'

'I imagine the fifth years are busy working for their G.C.S.E.'s,' said Miss Wrench. 'And of course the sixth formers are auditioning to get into companies and so forth.'

'Won't you let us do the show?' Cassie pressed her. 'It helps keep the blues away.'

'All right. I'll agree to this, but *only* this,' said Miss Wrench. 'All thoughts of fund-raising must stop.'

'Oh, thank you!' Cassie breathed. 'Thank you, thank you! You won't regret this, I promise.'

'You seem to be making quite a few promises,' said the Principal, with a wry smile. 'Just see that you keep them.'

7

A Secret Panel

Although disappointed they were not allowed to raise any more money, the action group threw itself wholeheartedly into organising and rehearsing the Gala, which had now added a tap number, led by Becky, to its programme. Cassie recognised that all the students who were involved in the Gala were in far better spirits than those who weren't. Even Emily, who had been more emotional than anyone at first, was focusing a vast amount of energy on her role as Cinderella. Even so, she still found at least an hour a day to play her flute.

'When I think how you used to spend every minute in the *dance* practice rooms!' Cassie said to her one day, when the girls were getting ready for character class.

'I know,' said Emily. 'I think it was the disappointment of Redwood closing and thinking I wouldn't get to dance Cinderella. The flute was such a comfort while I was ill.'

'Are you going off the idea of becoming a dancer, then?' asked Cassie.

Emily put down her hair-brush. 'I'm just confused, I think. I don't know whether I shall be able to go to another school, so, in case I can't, I want to carry on studying music.'

'I feel unsure too,' Cassie confided. 'I try not to think about next term and where I shall be, but I do know I still want to be a dancer, more than anything else in the world.'

'Then you'll probably make it,' said Emily. 'They say it's ten per cent talent, ninety per cent determination, don't they? I just don't think I've got your sticking-power!'

'Come on,' said Becky, doing a twirl in her full black skirt. 'We'll be late for class.'

Emily and Cassie put the finishing touches to their hair, sprayed it in place, and slipped on their black character shoes.

'I've been really glad of character and tap lessons this last few weeks,' said Cassie.

'How do you mean?' asked Poppy.

'Well, all the other teachers are so down in the dumps, aren't they? And Miss Oakland's in a right state about our exam. You'd think we were all going to fail, the way she goes on.'

'Yes, thank heavens for Mr Whistler,' said Becky admiringly.

'And Mrs Bonsing,' added Cassie. 'She's always good-humoured.'

'When you think about it,' said Emily, 'the staff must be just as anxious as we are. I mean, they'll have to look for other jobs. It can't be easy, especially for the ballet staff.'

'I've heard a rumour that Madame will retire early, rather than go elsewhere,' said Poppy.

'What about Miss Wrench, I wonder?' Cassie mused. 'It's hard to imagine her as anything else except Principal of Redwood Ballet School.'

Having finished their preparations, the girls made their way across to the main school for their character lesson.

'Good afternoon girls,' Mrs Bonsing called cheerfully as they entered the studio.

They curtseyed to her, as they wished her good afternoon, and began practising the Mazurka she was teaching them.

Cassie really enjoyed the class. Again, she was able to let her mind empty itself of all worries. She wouldn't let anything spoil her enjoyment of dance.

Cassie had worked very hard physically all day, and was beginning to feel ravenously hungry. Supper always seemed to be a long time after lunch, but today it was going to be later than ever, as she had an interview first with Miss Eiseldown.

She was seeing all her girls individually, to give

them advice about alternative schools. Cassie found her in the maths room.

'Ah, Cassandra,' she said. 'I have a couple of prospectuses here for schools I think would suit you. They're both in London.'

Cassie took the booklets and sat down. 'My parents haven't decided yet if they can afford the fees of another ballet school,' she said, 'so I can't really do much at the moment.'

'Oh, I see,' said Miss Eiseldown. 'Well, leave it with me. I'll look into the private girls' schools in your area. They often have ballet and drama on the curriculum, and the fees would be much less than if you were boarding.'

'Thank you, Miss Eiseldown,' Cassie said politely, but without enthusiasm.

Her house-mother sighed. 'This is going to be quite a blow for you, isn't it?'

Cassie shrugged. She didn't feel like opening her heart just at this moment. 'I'm concentrating my energies on the Gala and my exam now. If I think further ahead than that, it will drive me crazy.'

'Well, come to me any time you want to talk, don't forget.'

Cassie thanked her and went out, leaving the prospectuses on Miss Eiseldown's chair.

When she got to the dining-hall, the others had nearly finished their meals. Cassie tucked into an extra-large helping of spaghetti bolognese.

'It would be spaghetti,' she complained to her friends. 'I can never get the hang of keeping it on my fork.'

Becky laughed. 'We'd better stoke up well. We've got our own rehearsal straight after supper.'

'I'm not coming straight away,' said Cassie. 'Ask Marianne to start with the tap number and the fourth years' contemporary dance.'

'Why?' asked Becky.

'I've got to do some practice for my exam,' said Cassie. 'But I'll come along later.'

'We haven't really got enough items yet for the show,' said Poppy. 'Have you had any more ideas?'

'Not really,' said Cassie. 'I don't seem to get time to think.'

'I'll feed the cats on my own tonight if you like,' said Becky generously.

'I'll come with you for a change,' Poppy volunteered.

'Thanks,' said Cassie. 'That would give me a bit more practice time.'

'Perhaps it's just as well Miss Wrench stopped us doing any more fund-raising,' said Emily. 'We'd have been exhausted!'

'I enjoyed selling the badges,' Cassie said. 'If miserable old Mr Blane hadn't spotted us and objected, we wouldn't have had to stop!'

'He might not be miserable or old,' Becky pointed out. 'Actually, we probably met him – he must have come up close to us to read the badges.'

'Mmm, I wonder who he is,' said Cassie. 'I'd like to know a bit more about him.'

'It's hard to know why he was objecting,' said Emily. 'We could ask Madame if she knows anything about him.'

Cassie took up Emily's suggestion the next day, but Madame had little information about him, as he was new to the board of Trustees. She suggested asking Ojo's father, who was also a trustee of the school. Cassie went over to Matthew in the maths lesson which followed ballet class, to ask him for Ojo's address. When she explained the reason, Matthew offered to write the letter himself.

'I've been meaning to drop him a line anyway,' he said.

'Can you do it today?' asked Cassie.

'Oh, you always were bossy,' laughed Matthew. 'I'll do my best. What's the hurry though?'

'I just want to clear up something that's been bothering me: why should a trustee want to stop us from trying to save the school?'

'Well, for one thing, he knows it's a hopeless task and, for another, he probably thinks it isn't lady-like selling badges in the street. Lets the image of the school down, that sort of attitude.'

Cassie snorted. 'It's a bit late in the day to be worried about the school's image, isn't it? And if a few of you boys had joined the action group, we could have sent you down the street instead.'

Matthew chuckled. 'You never give in, do you, Cassie? But don't worry, I'll write to Ojo.'

'Today?'

'Today!'

Strolling round the grounds with Emily at lunch-time, Cassie was surprised to see Mr Smithson, the surveyor, inspecting the outside of the main building.

'I thought we'd seen the last of him!' she exclaimed.

It wasn't until the following day that she recalled the sighting. Mr Whistler had taken them for a very energetic tap lesson. Cassie and her friends stood sweating and panting at the end, when the young teacher came over to them, frowning.

'I thought you might like to hear the latest news,' he said, 'but don't spread it around please. It's not official.'

'What is it?' asked Cassie.

'Well, the surveyor has been back for a look at the building, and he reckons the signs of instability are worsening.'

'What does that mean?' asked Poppy.

'It may collapse rather sooner than they thought. We might all have to evacuate the school even before half-term, if he thinks it's become dangerous.'

Cassie's heart plunged. She couldn't believe her ears.

'He's coming back tomorrow, to do some more tests, but the future looks pretty bleak, I'm afraid.'

The friends wandered off to supper, barely able to accept this latest setback.

'Where does that leave the Gala?' said Becky.

'We must do it!' cried Cassie. 'Even if it means practising in a church hall.'

'But if we're sent home . . .?' said Emily.

'I don't know. We'll think of something.'

None of them had an appetite that evening. After pushing bean casserole round their plates for a while, the four of them set off to Mrs Allingham's to feed the cats.

'It's good to get outside,' said Cassie in the grounds. 'I feel that everything is pressing in on me in school.'

'Me too,' said Emily. 'I haven't even the heart to play my flute.'

As usual Tinker and Marmalade greeted them excitedly.

'They really look forward to our visits,' said Becky. 'It's not just the food – they need a bit of company too.'

'Oh, if only Mrs Allingham would hurry up and get better,' said Cassie. 'I thought she'd have been home by now.'

'I suppose it takes older people longer to get over a stroke,' said Becky.

They fed the cats and tidied up. The cottage felt lonely and cheerless without their friend there. The four girls walked back across the lawns in silence.

As they passed their old wing, Cassie had a sudden impulse.

'Let's go in!' she cried. 'It might be the last opportunity to see our old room and say goodbye to it.'

'It's bound to be locked,' said Emily. 'You can't get into it from the main building.'

'Let's try the back entrance,' Cassie said.

They went round to the back of the wing and tried the door, but it was locked. Cassie never gave up easily, however. She walked along the outer wall, trying each window.

'What do you think you're doing?' hissed Becky.

'Trying to find a window that's not properly on the catch.'

'Oh, Cassie!' moaned Becky. 'You'll get us all into trouble again!'

'What have we got to lose!' cried Cassie, her eyes glistening. 'I want to see Room 12 again!'

Her persistence paid off: the sixth window she tried wasn't fastened. She pushed up the lower pane and scrambled into the empty bedroom.

'Come on!' she called to the others. 'No one will see us.'

Soon the four girls were making their way upstairs to their old landing. They spent a couple of minutes in Room 12, but it didn't bring much comfort to any of them, least of all Cassie. Without furniture or the girls' own bits and pieces, it didn't have any connection with them any more.

'Let's explore upstairs,' said Cassie, trying to get away from the hollow feeling inside her.

'I think we should go back now,' said Emily nervously. 'This wing is supposed to be the most dangerous bit of the school.'

'Oh, nothing will happen,' said Cassie impatiently. 'I'm going up to the next floor anyway. On my own or not!'

Her friends sighed and followed Cassie upstairs. Spirits low, they tramped in and out of empty bedrooms, including the old staff study-bedrooms, and came to rest in Miss Oakland's old room.

'Do you remember the Unders and Overs race?' cried Cassie.

It seemed another lifetime when they had run that exciting, hair-raising race through the attics and cellars of the school.

'How could I ever forget!' Poppy replied.

Cassie began to laugh as she looked up at the ceiling, and remembered Poppy's foot dangling through it. She had lost her footing in the attic during the race and burst through Miss Oakland's ceiling.

'It wasn't funny at the time,' said Poppy, also beginning to giggle. 'I was stuck up there for hours!'

Cassie doubled over with laughter and collapsed against the wall, helpless. As she did so, the wooden panel opened inward and she fell backwards into a dark recess.

'How did you do that?' asked Becky.

'I don't know,' Cassie said, picking herself up and staring out at her friends.

'It must be a secret panel!' Cassie turned to explore the recess. It was a very small, windowless room. There was only room for two people inside, and even that was a squash. Its only feature was a narrow ledge which showed the remains of dripping candlewax.

'I reckon it hasn't been opened for years,' Cassie said, sniffing the musty air. 'Just think! A secret room! And Miss Oakland probably never suspected, the whole time she lived here.'

This thought made everyone feel much more excited. 'What could it have been used for?' Emily asked.

'A broom cupboard?' suggested Becky.

'Don't be daft,' said Cassie. 'You don't hide brooms behind secret panels.'

'It's big enough to hide a person,' said Poppy.

'I've got it!' cried Cassie. 'It's a priests' hole. You know, when priests were being persecuted in the seventeenth century, they used to hide in little places like this, didn't they?'

'You could be right,' said Becky. 'How marvellous that we've found it!'

Emily looked at her watch. 'I hate to spoil the fun, but I really think we should be getting back now.'

'I'll just go in for a last look,' said Cassie.

As her eyes grew accustomed to the dim light, she noticed that there was no plastered ceiling above her head, just rough joists. A pale object caught her eye, tucked behind a joist. She pulled at the corner of it, stretching on tiptoe, expecting it to be some forgotten scrap of waste paper. But when she took it in her hands, Cassie realised that it was a soft-covered notebook. She opened it carefully; the pages felt slightly crisp, as though they might tear easily. There was no doubt in her mind that the book had lain hidden for a very long time.

Cassie gave a soft whistle as she turned the pages. Before her eyes swam strange symbols. In the half-light of the priests' hole, they appeared to her like magical runes. With trembling fingers, she turned the leaves of the notebook. On every page it was the same.

Had this been the scene of witchcraft and sorcery? Cassie wondered excitedly.

'Hurry up, Cassie,' an impatient voice called,

snapping Cassie back to the present.

'Look!' Cassie cried. 'Look what I've found!'

Emily peered over her shoulder, as Cassie carefully leafed through the notebook. 'It's all in dance notation!' Emily said in surprise.

Dance notation wasn't quite as exciting as magic runes, but Cassie was not going to let her disappointment show. She turned back to the cover. It was quite faded and half-torn. Only some letters remained of the title and even fewer of the author's name.

UTY AND THE BE
BY ISA

'Oh, I love a good mystery!' cried Cassie. 'We'll take it back with us, and have a proper look at it later.'

With a good deal of effort they managed to pull the panel back into place. 'Phew! I didn't think we'd manage to close it again,' said Becky.

'It wouldn't have mattered. No one comes up here now,' said Poppy.

'You can't be too careful. This must be our secret!' said Cassie. 'Oh, this has cheered me up no end!'

8

Beauty and the Beast

The friends spent the rest of the evening examining the mysterious notebook. They quickly learned that the ballet was based on the story of *Beauty and the Beast*.

'That tells us what the title should say,' said Emily, repeating the letters 'UTY AND THE BEA', 'but we still don't know who wrote it.'

'What name could begin with ISA?' Cassie mused. 'Isadora? Isaiah?'

'Isabel?' suggested Becky.

'Anybody heard of a choreographer with any of those Christian names?' asked Cassie.

'Isadora Duncan,' said Emily.

'It's not her kind of dancing,' said Cassie. 'This is definitely ballet. Oh how I wish Mrs Allingham were at home. We could have asked her!'

'I wonder how the notebook got there?' asked Poppy.

'And how long it's been there,' added Becky.

'Well, it's not hundreds of years old, is it?' said Cassie. 'But I should think it's been there quite a long time.'

She flicked through the pages once more, this time opening a folded sheet of paper tucked inside the back cover. 'Here's a handwritten message!' she exclaimed.

Her friends crowded round to peer at the message, but Cassie, relishing the drama of it all, read it aloud:

I fear my old persecutors have tracked me down – even to this sceptred isle. They might capture me, but they won't have my ballet – the last child of my heart.

Cherish it as you would an orphan.

I.Z. 1944

The girls shivered. 'Poor man – if it is a man,' said Cassie.

'I wonder who was after him?' said Poppy.

'Goodness knows,' Cassie answered. 'But wait a minute! The date. 1944! That was during the second world war.'

'Yes, but how does that explain why he was hiding at Redwood?' asked Becky.

88

'I don't know,' Cassie cried, 'but we must find out!'

'Perhaps he was quite important,' Emily suggested.

'Maybe,' said Cassie thoughtfully.

Even after lights out, the girls went on chattering in hushed whispers about their find.

The next morning, they all felt tired, their spirits deflated, and their temporary excitement gone. The latest news on Redwood's fate came flooding back to them.

The girls couldn't fail to notice the ominous presence of Mr Smithson, the sandy-haired surveyor, taking more measurements and tests round the buildings. They passed him several times during the morning.

When they returned to Room 13 after lessons had finished, they bumped into Miss Eiseldown, on her way out.

'There's a special assembly, girls,' she explained. 'Come down to the hall straight away.'

She walked down the corridor, relaying the message to all the girls who lived on that floor.

'I'm surprised she didn't ask us what we were doing wandering about after supper,' said Becky.

'She looked as though she had other things on her mind,' Emily pointed out. 'We'd better get down to assembly.'

The Deputy Principal, who taught geography, was in charge while the whole school – Junior, Senior and sixth form – packed into the hall. Cassie gazed up at the stained-glass windows above the rostrum and the school crest which hung on the wall. She guessed that they were to hear the bad news that Mr Whistler had foretold. How strange to imagine this great hall standing silent and empty, instead of bursting with young people as it was now.

Miss Wrench walked on to the rostrum with a weary air. As she scanned the faces in front of her, a hush fell upon the hall.

'I have an important and sad announcement to make,' she said. 'The building is now believed to be in a more dangerous condition than we at first thought. Your safety must be our prime consideration, and so the school will be closed at the end of next week. Parents will be allowed to collect you at any time before that, if they prefer.'

Although Cassie had seen it coming, hearing the announcement from Miss Wrench's lips made it sound final and absolute.

The school sat in a state of shock while the Principal read out some further notices. At the end of the assembly she asked Cassie, Emily, Becky and Poppy to remain behind.

As the rest of the school filed out, the friends waited at the foot of the rostrum. Miss Wrench was still standing, staring blankly into the depths of the hall.

'I wonder if it's about the Gala?' Emily whispered to Cassie.

The last few stragglers left the hall, but still their Principal stood, staring into space. She seemed to have forgotten all about them.

Cassie coughed loudly. Miss Wrench turned towards them with a start.

'Come up, please,' she ordered.

They joined her on the rostrum, and she sat down at her desk, looking up at them sharply.

'You were seen climbing through a window of the girls' wing last night,' she said.

Cassie hadn't expected this. Her stomach lurched with fright.

'I thought I'd made it quite clear that the girls' wing is out of bounds. The building is dangerous!'

'Yes, Miss Wrench,' the girls chorused.

'While I am Principal of this school,' she paused, her eyes clouding over ' – I expect my students to obey the rules. I really take a very dim view of such reckless behaviour. You may think it no longer matters, but I assure you it does. How can we give good references to students who flout the rules? And what about your safety? Whilst you are at this school, your physical well-being is my responsibility.'

Cassie looked at her feet. She felt very uncomfortable. Her impulsive behaviour might have harmed not only herself, but her friends too.

'I'm terribly sorry, Miss Wrench,' she said. 'It was my suggestion. Please don't punish the others for it. I just wanted to see our old room, that's all.'

Miss Wrench looked at her sternly. 'I actually believed you were developing into a more mature, responsible student! Now I see that the old Cassandra is still very much in evidence! You have let me down and led your friends into something their better judgement should have told them not to get involved in.'

91

Cassie stood with her chin bravely jutting out, but inwardly she was quaking. What could she do to stop his tirade?

An idea came to her.

'We found something really interesting while we were exploring Miss Oakland's old room,' Cassie blurted out. 'An old notebook with notations for a ballet written in it. We think it's for *Beauty and the Beast*.'

The Principal was taken aback. As Cassie had hoped, Miss Wrench's curiosity about the notebook drowned her anger.

'Where was it?' she asked.

'Behind a secret panel,' Cassie said. 'There was a sort of priests' hole behind it.'

'Go and fetch it!' commanded Miss Wrench.

Cassie was all too happy to leave the tense atmosphere on the rostrum. At least she was reprieved for the few minutes it took her to walk across to the boys' block and back. On her return, she met Becky, Poppy and Emily.

'Good luck!' whispered Becky. 'She's let us go, but she is going to decide on a punishment tomorrow morning.'

'Why did you tell her about the secret panel?' asked Poppy.

'If Redwood is closing anyway, there's not much point in keeping it secret any longer,' Cassie replied.

'No, I suppose not,' agreed Poppy.

Cassie mounted the rostrum once more and held out the notebook with trembling hands.

Miss Wrench studied it eagerly through her flat-topped reading glasses.

'Well, I agree it's *Beauty and the Beast*,' she said. 'Unknown to me, I'm afraid.'

'Please, Miss Wrench. There's a folded piece of paper at the back with a very strange message written on it.'

The Principal found the message and read it carefully. Her face blanched as she looked up at Cassie.

'It's just possible that I.Z. stands for Isaac Zimmerman!' she cried.

Cassie was thrilled. Izaac Zimmerman had been a world-famous choreographer.

'He was a Polish Jew,' Miss Wrench went on, with mounting excitement in her voice, 'but I had no idea he had ever visited Redwood!'

'Do you think he was captured here?' asked Cassie.

'The message makes it seem that way,' Miss Wrench answered. 'Poor man, he must have felt like a hunted animal!'

Miss Wrench collected herself and focused her steely eyes on Cassie.

'I want to make it quite clear to you, Cassandra, that the girls' wing is *absolutely out of bounds* from now on.'

'Yes, Miss Wrench.'

'However, I can't pretend I'm sorry you found this extraordinary notebook. To think it might be the last known work of a very great choreographer!'

The Principal's eyes had begun to sparkle. A question that had been uppermost in Cassie's mind

93

for the last few minutes burst out of her uncontrollably.

'Is it worth a lot of money?'

'Well, of course, we shall have to get experts to look at it, but if it is genuinely written by Zimmerman, then it will be worth several thousand pounds!'

'Fantastic!' Cassie exclaimed. 'And to think this ballet has been lying up there all those years. Perhaps we were meant to find it.'

'What do you mean, Cassandra?'

'Well, it's come at just the right time, hasn't it?'

'I see what you're implying. But we mustn't let our excitement run away with us. The experts will have to decide.'

Despite Miss Wrench's caution, and the fact that there was no announcement over the next few days to contradict the imminent closure of the school, Cassie was convinced that the notebook was to be Redwood's saviour. She sought permission to photocopy the ballet notes and with the help of Marianne and Madame Larette, marked out the dances of the ballet.

'What are we doing this for?' asked Marianne, the next day when they were working out the dances of the last act, with Emily and Poppy.

'I've had a great idea,' said Cassie. 'I think we should include *Beauty and the Beast* in our Gala. We could give it its world premiere!'

'But Cassie,' Emily remonstrated, 'we close at the end of this week. There isn't going to be a Gala!'

'Oh yes there is,' said Cassie firmly.

* * *

Immediately after breakfast, another assembly was called.

'About time too,' Cassie whispered to Emily.

'Do you think it will really be good news?'

'Of course,' said Cassie.

Cassie was right. Miss Wrench announced a postponement of the school's closure, explaining about the discovery of the notebook.

'It has now been confirmed,' she said, 'that the choreographer *is* Isaac Zimmerman and the proceeds from the sale of the notebook will be used to shore up the main school, providing enough scaffolding to make it safe for the time being. I have informed all your parents by letter. We should now be able to see out the end of this term, at least.'

In her heart of hearts, Cassie had been hoping that the notebook would fetch the quarter of a million that Redwood needed. Disappointed on that score, she was nonetheless relieved that they would, at any rate, be able to see the Gala performance.

Cassie cajoled everyone into continuing rehearsals for the show. They also began to practise *Beauty and the Beast* with Madame's help. There were no formal auditions and by popular vote Cassie was chosen to dance Beauty and Matthew the Beast.

'I'm used to the role,' he joked after the first rehearsal.

'There are some wonderful dances for both of us, aren't there?' Cassie mused, delighted to be able to concentrate on dancing, rather than the gloomy future of Redwood.

Madame came over to them. 'It is most fascinating to see how the ballet develops,' she said. 'You are very fortunate to 'ave the chance to dance it first.'

'Do you think it is by Zimmerman, Madame?' Cassie asked her.

'There is no doubt in my mind *ma cherie*. It 'as every 'allmark of 'is work.'

When the friends were back in their room that night, Cassie admitted that she felt exhausted.

'I'm not surprised,' said Becky. 'Think about all the extra work you're doing for the Gala and your exam. You've even had a whole new ballet to tackle. I'm surprised you're not flat on your back really.'

'I am now,' said Cassie, flopping back on her bed. 'I just wish Miss Wrench would hurry up and tell us what the experts have to say about Isaac Zimmerman and what he was doing at Redwood.'

'You know what experts are like,' said Becky.

'I can't think about anything much at the moment except our exam,' said Emily. 'It seems to have come round so quickly.'

'No,' sighed Poppy. 'I don't feel ready for it, and with everything up in the air, it's so hard to get down to serious work.'

'Well, you've got precisely three days,' said Emily. 'So you'd better get down to it pretty sharpish!'

'Some people leave everything till the last minute!' added Celia, none too kindly.

Celia was in a mood, because Cassie and the others had given her only a minor part in *Beauty and the Beast*.

'And I don't know why we're bothering to learn

Beauty and the Beast,' she went on. 'Miss Wrench will probably change her mind again and close the school before we can put it on stage!'

'Well, no one's making you take part,' Cassie countered.

'And while we're on the subject, I really don't think it's fair that you've given Jane a bigger part than me. She is leaving after all, which proves I'm better.'

'We're all leaving at some point,' said Cassie, 'unless our notebook's worth a lot more than Miss Wrench thought.'

Cassie slept like a log that night, but woke still feeling tired. All her problems and responsibilities were spinning round her head. She had had a vivid dream about Mrs Allingham, which had stirred up her anxieties.

Later, in ballet class, she made herself concentrate hard. Passing her exam with a high mark was really important, whether she stayed at Redwood or not. However, her legs felt sluggish, and Miss Oakland reprimanded her several times for minor errors. Frustratingly, Cassie's legs wouldn't do what she asked of them.

Extra practice after lunch didn't seem to improve matters.

'You need a rest, Cassie,' said Emily, coming into the practice room to join her. 'You're doing too much!'

But Cassie was committed to a hectic schedule of rehearsals squeezed into the short periods available to them. As the Gala came together, so Cassie's exam preparation seemed to come apart.

9

Missing Leotards

The evening before the exam, Cassie called in at the laundry room to pick up her clean leotards. She would need one for the next day. She found her name label, but no laundry. Matron could shed no light on its disappearance.

'But what shall I do?' cried Cassie. 'I've got my exam tomorrow and no clean uniform!'

Matron went scurrying round the room in a fluster, but still could not find them.

'Someone must have taken them!' Cassie declared, when she got back to Room 13.

'Whoever it was got their timing just right!' Poppy remarked. 'I can't offer to help out, as I've only one clean leotard left myself.'

'Mine and Emily's wouldn't fit you,' said Becky. 'You're so much taller.'

'I don't know what to do,' said Cassie, nearly in tears. 'I can't appear in this one. It looks really grotty.'

'Go to Miss Eiseldown,' suggested Emily. 'I'll come with you.'

On their way across to the main building, Cassie racked her brains as to who might have pinched her leotards.

'Matthew did it once before,' she said.

'But not this time,' said Emily. 'He's taking his exam too, and he knows how wound up you get.'

'What about Celia?' Cassie asked.

'She is pretty cross about Jane having a bigger part. You may be right. But it's better not to have a scene with her just before your exam.'

As they crossed the tarmac square, Cassie heard her name being called. She turned. Abigail was running after them, and they waited for her to catch up.

'I've found your leotards,' she panted.

'Where?' asked Cassie.

'In the wardrobe,' Abigail replied, 'when I was putting some of my things away.'

'Any idea who put them there?' asked Cassie.

'It must have been Celia,' said Abigail. 'They were under a pile of her stuff.'

'Well, that explains it,' said Cassie. 'I'll kill Celia when I see her.'

'Don't tell Celia it was me who found them,' Abigail said.

'We'll have to see what we can do about Celia,' said Cassie, seething inwardly.

'Not now,' said Emily anxiously. 'It's your exam in the morning, remember. The last thing you want is a major bust-up.'

'No, I won't do anything yet,' said Cassie. 'Just make plans – that can be pretty satisfying.'

'Don't be too hard on her,' said Abigail.

'No. And thanks Abi – you've saved my day,' said Cassie, smiling.

'Well, I'm just glad it won't be a panic for you tomorrow.'

Cassie struggled to fall asleep that night; was she properly prepared for her Elementary exam, she wondered?

In the wink of an eye, it seemed, the morning was upon her. She rose an hour early to give herself time to run through the complete syllabus before breakfast.

'You're an early bird,' said Emily as she passed her practice room. Cassie had left the door open.

'How are you feeling, Em?' Cassie called cheerfully. She was more wide awake than she had been for days.

'Nervous,' laughed Emily. 'Poppy and Abi are too.'

Their exams were scheduled through the morning, so they would miss ballet class.

Cassie went into her exam with her mind less troubled than lately. A feeling of calm descended on her, enabling her to use her brains as well as her body to the best advantage. There was some quite difficult pointe work at the Elementary level. Footwork had to be crisp and strong throughout. Cassie was relieved to feel in control of her legs and feet once more, but was horrified when, during echappés en croix, which she normally found easy, she forgot to change feet after the echappé à la seconde. After that, she had to watch herself like a hawk to prevent other careless slips.

She turned her pirouettes beautifully, with two turns apiece, and even managed one which ended in attitude very gracefully.

Towards the end of the exam, tiredness began to hit her. Cassie knew she didn't do so well in the Batterie section. She came out of the exam room quite unable to judge what mark she might have been given.

Comparing notes with Emily later, they both realised that it was much more difficult in these major exams to reach the very high marks they used to obtain in the grade exams. The work was so much more complex and demanding.

'I saw Matthew after his exam,' said Emily.

'How did he think he'd got on?'

'Quite well, I think. He said he had some news for you.'

When they saw Matthew at lunch-time he told them he'd had a reply from Ojo, about the school trustee, Mr Blane. It turned out that he lived in the village close to Redwood. Ojo even supplied his address.

'That's convenient!' said Carrie. 'Next Saturday we'll

have a walk down to the village, and take a peep at his house.'

'What for?' asked Becky.

'Curiosity,' said Cassie. 'You never know what we may discover.'

'Have we got time to nip across to Mrs Allingham's?' asked Becky. 'We're going to be so busy tonight with rehearsals, I thought we'd better feed the cats early.'

Cassie agreed and they walked across the grounds to the cottage together. There was no longer that warm feeling of anticipation in their visits. If the cats had not been there, they wouldn't have gone at all. The emptiness of the cottage always upset them, reminding them as it did of Mrs Allingham's absence.

'She's taking ages and ages to get better,' sighed Cassie, as they fed Tinker and Marmalade.

'I'm beginning to wonder if she'll ever come back,' said Becky sadly.

'Oh, don't say that!' said Cassie sharply. 'Whenever we visit her, her eyes twinkle. And she always wants to know all the Redwood gossip.'

'We haven't told her about the notebook yet,' said Becky.

'Well, we can tell her when we visit on Thursday night,' said Cassie. 'She'll be thrilled!'

When the girls got back to their block, a fourth year was waiting for them in Room 13, along with Poppy and Emily.

'Miss Wrench wants to see you,' said the older girl.

The four friends followed her across to the main building and through the school to the Principal's study. Cassie stared at the panelled door, wondering if this was to be good news or bad.

The study door opened and they were ushered in. 'Thank you for coming girls,' said Miss Wrench.

This sounds promising, thought Cassie, as she dropped a curtsey.

'I thought you might like to hear what the experts have come up with about Isaac Zimmerman.'

Cassie's ears pricked up.

'We were right in thinking he was being pursued when he came to Redwood,' said Miss Wrench. 'I think I mentioned before that he was a Polish Jew?'

The girls nodded.

'At the height of his fame, the Nazis came to power. He was immediately made one of their targets. He fled Poland but was pursued across Europe to England.'

'And that's when he hid in the priests' hole?' asked Cassie.

'Yes, that's right,' Miss Wrench replied. 'The Principal of the school at that time was a good friend of his. She sheltered him here, but one night his pursuers came whilst everyone was fast asleep and abducted him.'

'Did they kill him?' asked Becky, eyes wide with suspense.

'We think so, but his body was never recovered.'

Cassie felt a chill run down her spine. 'Well, I'm really glad *we* found his notebook and not the Nazis,' she said.

'It was obviously very precious to him,' Miss Wrench

agreed. 'Well, you'd better run along to your lesson now. I hear from Madame that rehearsals for *Beauty and the Beast* are going very well.'

'Yes. Thank you Miss Wrench,' replied Cassie.

The four girls dashed out of Miss Wrench's office, excitedly discussing the notebook.

Later in the afternoon, despite her near-exhaustion, Cassie had a rehearsal of *Beauty and the Beast*. Madame was too busy to attend, so Marianne was directing. She had a flair for organising people and managed to make useful criticisms without upsetting anyone. Anyone, that is, except Celia.

In Celia's small role as a villager, she had a short sequence when she danced alone. She was supposed to be bringing the others news of Beauty's disappearance, and some of her part involved mime. Marianne stopped her during her first run-through.

'Celia, you must be more expressive. Use your face and hands to convey your meaning!'

'What do you know about it!' Celia cried. 'You're only one of us!'

'If you want to be part of this, then you must listen to criticism,' said Marianne patiently.

'I'll listen to Madame!' Celia snapped.

Marianne sighed and continued with the rehearsal. At the end of Act One, she took Cassie on one side. 'I don't know what we should do about Celia,' she said. 'She causes a lot of trouble!'

'I'll have a word with Madame about her tomorrow,' said Cassie, pulling on her track suit. 'By the way,

Marianne, I think I've come up with a really good idea for the Gala.'

'Oh, what's that?'

'Well, as there might be quite a lot of interest in the new ballet, I thought we might get one of the Birmingham theatres to stage our Gala.'

'What a wonderful idea!' cried Marianne. She had just been unpinning her bun and shook out her long, red–gold hair, which gleamed in the rays of evening sun shining through the studio's sash-windows. 'Are you going to ask Madame?' she said.

'No,' said Cassie. 'I thought I'd try the theatres myself. It is *our* project, after all!'

'Best of luck!' said Marianne. 'You might find they're all booked up by now, though. Theatres work out their programmes months ahead.'

Cassie had to admit she hadn't thought of that, but decided to have a go anyway. Before she went to bed that night, she worked out a letter to send to the three main theatres in the city.

Before breakfast the next day she had written out three copies:

Redwood Ballet School
Birmingham

To the Theatre Manager

Dear Sir/Madam,

I wondered if you might have any free dates in your June programme? The reason I'm asking is because we have found this wonderful new ballet by Zimmerman called *Beauty and the Beast*, and we're putting it in our Gala. We thought lots of people, not just our parents, might want to come and watch it. We really want to sell a lot of tickets to raise money for our school, which will probably have to close at the end of term because it's falling down.

I do hope you can help us.

Yours sincerely,
CASSANDRA BROWN

Having addressed and sealed each envelope, Cassie kissed them for luck.

'It's probably a waste of time,' she said to Becky, who was getting her school bag ready for the morning's lessons.

'Nothing ventured, nothing gained,' said Becky. 'Have you decided what you're going to do about Celia yet?'

Cassie giggled. 'Do you fancy looking for some worms with me?'

Becky's eyes lit up. 'This will be quite like old times. We'll go to the rose garden at lunch-time. There's a flower-bed the gardeners have just dug over. Perfect for worms!'

Lunch-time found the two girls with a ruler and an empty toffee tin, digging in the flower-bed. They had a tinful of worms within a few minutes.

'Are they going in her bed?' Becky asked, as they sauntered back to school.

'Yes,' Cassie said. 'Let's find the others. They can check that Celia's out of the way.'

It was getting towards the end of the lunch-hour when they saw Poppy.

'Where's Emily?' asked Cassie.

'She's at orchestra,' Poppy said.

'Orchestra!' cried Becky and Cassie. They had completely forgotten their rehearsal. There was to be a recital in the local church just after half-term, which involved the school orchestra and various soloists.

'Oh no!' groaned Cassie. 'Mr Green will be furious.'

'We'd better go straight across and apologise,' said Becky.

'Before or after the worms?'

'No, we *must* get across to the music room before the end of the lunch-hour!' cried Becky consulting her watch.

'Well, give me the worms,' said Poppy. 'I'll do it.'

'No, it's OK,' said Cassie. 'I want the pleasure of doing it myself!'

Mr Green listened to their apologies with a frown.

'You must take your school commitments more seriously,' he told them. 'You know full well that we have a recital very soon.'

Emily, who had been packing away her flute, approached them and did her best to divert the music teacher from being cross with her friends.

'Was my phrasing all right, Mr Green?' she asked.

'Oh yes, Emily, it was very good indeed.' He beamed at her. 'You'll be our star turn, you know.'

Cassie and Becky took their opportunity to slip away.

'It's amazing how Emily has become so brilliant on the flute!' said Becky.

'I know,' said Cassie. 'I bet her parents will feel really

proud of her when she plays at the church.'

'We haven't got time to go back to our room now,' said Becky.

'Keep the tin in your school bag,' said Cassie. 'We may get a chance during preparation if Celia goes to work in a study room.'

Their last lesson before preparation was geography with Mr Watson, the Deputy Principal. He was a strict and humourless teacher who had very exacting standards.

He was walking round the classroom, checking the maps of Europe they were copying into their exercise books. He stopped beside Becky and Cassie.

'How many times have I told you, Rebecca, not to use felt tip pens on your work? Coloured pencils are so much neater!'

'Sorry, Mr Watson,' Becky said. She reached into her bag to take out her pack of colouring pencils, knocking the tin as she did so. It clattered on to the floor, and the lid came off.

By the time Mr Watson had returned to see what had happened, there was a squiggly mass of worms on the floor.

'Good heavens!' he cried. 'Where did they come from?'

Becky's bright red face gave him the answer.

'G . . . get them out of here at once!' he spluttered. 'And take a detention!'

Becky scooped the worms back into the tin and hurried out of the classroom. She did not return as quickly as Cassie expected.

'Where've you been?' she whispered, when Becky sat down again, puffing.

'Took a detour!' Becky whispered, grinning.

Celia didn't suspect anything until she climbed into bed that night and encountered the worms with her bare feet. As Cassie listened to her shrieks, she felt avenged.

'You did this, didn't you?' Celia demanded, striding up to Cassie's bed.

'You hid my leotards, didn't you?' Cassie retorted calmly.

'Of course I didn't!' Celia lied. 'Putting slugs and worms and things in people's beds is really babyish!'

'Not quite as babyish as hiding people's uniform,' said Cassie.

The following evening, Madame Larette was able to help them with their *Beauty and the Beast* rehearsal. Cassie had a quiet word with her about Celia before they began.

'I shall speak to Celia,' Madame promised. 'It is not fair on the rest of you if she is behaving badly.'

Madame kept her word. She took Celia on one side almost immediately and, although Cassie could not hear what she was saying, she could tell by her expression that Celia was not getting off lightly.

The rehearsal did not get off to a good start that night. Jane had some bad news for them. Her parents had booked a special holiday for the family in June.

'When in June?' asked Cassie. 'Perhaps we could avoid the dates you're away.'

'That's the trouble,' said Jane, sighing. 'It's for the whole month!'

'Oh no!' groaned Cassie. 'Do you have to go with them?'

Cassie knew she was being selfish but Jane had quite an important part in the ballet as the Spirit of the Rose, which symbolised the Beast's life-force.

'It's all booked. I didn't have any choice,' Jane replied. 'They thought it would cheer me up, you know, for having to leave Redwood and everything!'

'There's no question about it,' said Madame softly. 'You are being given a very special treat, Jane. You must go. We will manage without you.'

Cassie looked round the room. Who would they be able to put in the part? Becky was the Beast's housekeeper, a comic role with not very much classical dancing. The fourth year girls had taken on the important male roles, as there had been a lack of boys volunteering. Poppy was Beauty's sister. Emily was only a villager, but she was dancing the leading role in *Cinderella*.

Then Cassie noticed Celia's expression. She could tell that she was expecting the part.

Madame was very tactful. 'I leave it to you to decide,' she said to Marianne and Cassie. 'It is your ballet, after all!'

Cassie took Marianne over to a quiet corner.

'Do you think we should promote Celia?' asked Marianne.

'No!' said Cassie. 'Not after all the bother she's

111

caused. Let's give it to Emily – she would make a beautiful Rose!'

'You're right,' said Marianne. 'Emily it is!'

Emily was thrilled at the offer and was quite ready to accept the extra work it entailed.

'We might as well make the best use we can of our last few weeks here!' she said.

'Oh don't,' said Cassie. 'I can't bear to think it's really all going to come to an end!'

Celia didn't look at all happy. While Madame was present, she contained herself, but as soon as the teacher had gone, she exploded.

'I should have known better than to join this!' she shouted, her face turning red with fury. 'You're just giving the best parts to your friends. It's not fair at all! Well, I've had enough. You can count me out!'

She stalked off and slammed the studio door behind her.

'Well, perhaps that solves one of our problems,' said Marianne.

'Yes, good riddance,' said Poppy.

Just then, Mr Whistler popped his head round the door.

'Oh, you're still here!' he said. 'I thought I'd just look in to see how the ballet's shaping up.'

He came into the studio, looking puzzled. 'I was nearly flattened in the corridor by Celia,' he went on. 'She was like a steam-roller.'

'She's cross with us,' said Marianne. 'She hasn't got the part she wanted, so she's just quit!'

'Oh,' said Mr Whistler. 'So how is *Beauty and the Beast* coming on then?'

'Well, there's had to be a shake-up of parts today, but otherwise, fine,' Marianne answered.

'What about costumes, scenery, that sort of thing?'

'Madame's shown us some costumes in wardrobe which will do for the villagers and all the male parts, apart from the Beast. He'll need a costume and an elaborate mask. I don't know who's going to make them. Beauty and Rose will need really beautiful tutus. We haven't really thought about how we're going to pay for them.'

'It needs sorting out,' said Mr Whistler. 'Lack of money is often the thing that spoils everything. You'd better have a careful think about it over half term.'

Intuition prompted Cassie to ask her next question. 'Have you heard anything else about the school?'

'I shouldn't tell you really,' he said, 'but it'll be common knowledge soon, I suppose . . .'

'Oh tell us, Mr Whistler,' Cassie begged.

'Well, the Redwood estate is going to be sold at the end of July. The building is to be demolished and a housing estate built on the land.'

The girls looked at one another in horror. The news sounded so definite, so final. The end of their ballet school; it seemed inescapable now.

10

A Shock for Emily

After their half-term holiday, the friends returned to school refreshed but still rather dazed by Mr Whistler's news. On the first Saturday back, they sat about in their bedroom after lunch, staring glumly out of the window.

'We knew we were only going to stay open until the end of term,' said Emily, 'but somehow, the excitement about the notebook, and seeing all the workmen back propping up the main building made it seem as if it wasn't going to happen after all.'

'I still can't accept it,' said Cassie. 'If only we could find something else that would raise a lot of money!'

'Oh, you never give up, do you!' Becky exclaimed.

'You've got to face facts, Cassie.'

'I just can't,' said Cassie. 'I'm like Mrs Allingham – a fighter!' Cassie paused as she thought of her elderly friend still in hospital. Then, another thought slipped into her mind.

'While I was on holiday, I couldn't keep Mr Blane out of my mind. Do you fancy coming with me to have a look at his house?' she asked.

'Mr Blane!' exclaimed Poppy. 'How can he help us?'

'Just a hunch,' said Cassie. She felt they needed something to lift their spirits. Everyone was getting so depressed.

'I will,' said Becky.

'And me,' said Emily.

Later, with Miss Eiseldown's permission, they walked a little way out of the village's centre, found Mr Blane's road, and proceeded to look for his house, The Yews.

'Look out for some yew trees,' said Cassie.

They spotted some towards the end of the cul-de-sac and headed towards them. The Yews was the last house but one. A fir hedge edged the front garden, but the gate to the drive stood open.

Cassie could see a large, brass plate at the side of the front door. She made out the name 'R.G. BLANE', inscribed on the plate, but could not read the writing underneath.

'Dare we go down the drive?' she hissed.

'What for?' asked Becky.

'I want to read the plate.'

'I'm not going down,' said Emily, nervously.

Cassie peered through the fir hedge into the front room of the house, to see if she could see anyone about. She couldn't. Crossing her fingers, she nipped down the drive and stood in front of the porch, reading the plate.

She had just turned to go when the front door opened. A blonde, middle-aged woman, wearing expensive jewellery and reeking of perfume, stood there with a questioning frown.

'Did you want something?' she asked.

'Oh – er – yes, I didn't think there was anyone in,' said Cassie, racking her brains to think of an explanation.

The woman still looked at her suspiciously.

'Have you seen my pet rabbit?' Cassie said suddenly. 'He's escaped.'

'No, I've seen no rabbits,' the woman said impatiently.

'Oh, sorry to have bothered you,' said Cassie, and ran back to join her friends at the hedge.

'Well?' they asked. Cassie looked excited.

'It said he was a builder and property developer! Just suppose he's got something to do with building the new houses on our grounds!'

'There are loads of builders around,' Becky pointed out. 'I think we'd better move away. That woman's still staring at us out of her window.'

When they got back to school, they passed Mr Smithson, the surveyor, with his measuring tape.

'You'd have thought his job would be over now,' Cassie remarked to her friends, as they entered the boys' block.

'He can't seem to keep away!' said Emily. 'He gives Poppy the creeps, and I must say I don't like him either.'

As they reached Room 13, Cassie saw a note pinned to the door.

'It's for me!' she exclaimed.

CASSANDRA BROWN
PLEASE REPORT TO MISS WRENCH'S STUDY
IMMEDIATELY ON RETURN.

'That doesn't sound too good,' she said, taking it into the room with her.

'Don't worry,' said Emily. 'It's probably nothing important!'

Cassie felt her stomach tighten into a knot as she made her way to the Principal's study. What could have happened? Surely Mrs Blane – if that's who the blonde woman was – hadn't reported her?

Entering the study, Cassie could tell immediately that Miss Wrench wasn't very pleased with her. She dropped a curtsey and wished her good afternoon as sweetly as she knew how.

'I've had a phone call,' Miss Wrench began, 'which took me quite by surprise!'

It looked as though Cassie's guess had been correct. Miss Wrench paused and looked her full in the face.

'Cassandra, you really must learn not to take the law into your own hands. This is the second time this term you have done something impulsive without first seeking permission.'

Carrie was just about to burst out, 'But we did ask permission!' when the Principal continued, so she held her peace.

'The phone call was from the Birmingham Repertory Theatre. They tell me you wrote to them about the Gala.'

Cassie brightened visibly. 'What did they say?' she asked eagerly.

'Cassandra, I do admire your enthusiasm, but really, you should do these things through the proper channels.'

Cassie was still looking up expectantly.

'They said,' Miss Wrench continued, 'that they would offer the theatre for one night at the end of June for your Gala to take place.'

'Wow! That's terrific!' cried Cassie.

'I haven't given my permission yet,' said Miss Wrench, sternly. 'I'll come along to your rehearsal this evening. If the ballet has reached a good enough standard, then we'll see.'

'Oh, thank you, Miss Wrench,' said Cassie.

'If nothing else, it will be good publicity for the sale of the notebook, which is taking place in July. And of course it will be a feather in your cap, when you come to audition for a new school.'

Cassie hadn't quite thought of it that way. She was thrilled that they might get the opportunity to present the new ballet at the theatre, and couldn't wait to tell her friends about it.

'Gosh, we'd better be good at the rehearsal,' said Emily. 'I don't know my part very well yet.'

'I'll go over it with you now, if you like,' said Cassie. 'We should be able to find a practice room easily enough.'

Cassie enjoyed going over the delicate solo bits of the Spirit of the Rose. Emily had just the light, airy quality that the character needed, and she seemed much more confident after half an hour's intensive work. 'You know Beauty's part really well, don't you?' Emily remarked.

'Yes, I seemed to be able to pick it up quickly. It's just the pas de deux work that's a bit tricky, as always,' said Cassie. 'That one near the end is lovely, though. You know, when you think the Beast is dying.'

'Has Matthew got a mask yet?'

'No,' said Cassie. 'Miss Wrench may want to know about costumes. We need some money, but I'm sure the school can't afford any.'

Emily pondered the problem as she pulled her track suit on over her practice leotard. 'You know this concert we're doing in the church? Well, we're selling tickets for it. The money was going to school funds, but I don't suppose there's much point now, is there?'

'Ask Mr Green about it,' said Cassie, excitedly. 'Perhaps he'd be willing to give us what he raises for our production.'

The students felt nervous as they ran through *Beauty and the Beast*, with Miss Wrench's critical eye upon them. Madame had joined her, which gave Cassie a bit more confidence. Even so, she stumbled a few times in one of the pas de deux. Marianne looked more anxious than anyone, standing a little to one side of the two teachers, watching the results of her labours.

Miss Wrench turned to her first, at the end, and congratulated her on her efforts. Then she spoke to the cast.

'Well done, all of you. There are a few ragged edges, of course, but I have no doubt that this will be in good shape by the end of June. I shall inform the theatre today that we should like to take up their offer.'

There were cheers all round at Miss Wrench's decision. Marianne rushed over to Cassie and gave her a big hug.

'It was such a brilliant idea of yours,' she said, 'and now it's paid off. We'll show the city just what they're going to lose!'

Cassie and Emily were delighted when, at the next orchestra practice, Mr Green said he had decided to let them have the ticket-money for their Gala fund.

'That's marvellous, Mr Green,' said Cassie. 'Thank you!'

'On one condition,' said the music teacher, smiling. 'That you miss no more orchestra rehearsals.'

Their final rehearsal was in the church itself, the evening before the concert. It was a warm but windy night, and the girls enjoyed their walk to the village from school.

'I wonder if Mrs Blane's still looking for my pet rabbit?' said Cassie with a giggle, as they passed the end of her road.

'What rabbit?' Celia demanded. She had come up

behind them without their noticing.

'Just a joke,' said Cassie. 'Are you still playing that lovely cornet solo?' she asked, trying to change the subject.

'Yes,' said Celia. 'Of course I am, though I can't quite see why some people get to have two spots in the concert!'

She walked ahead huffily. 'Oh dear,' said Cassie. 'I've set her off again. I suppose she meant you, Emily.'

'I suppose she did,' said Emily, who had indeed been given two solo parts, as Mr Green was so pleased with her playing.

'She hasn't forgiven us yet about the Gala parts,' said Cassie.

'Oh, Celia's always cross about something!' said Emily. 'But I think she cut off her nose to spite her face when she dropped out of the Gala.'

'Yes, I bet she's kicking herself now it's going to be at the Birmingham Rep.,' said Cassie.

On arrival at the church, the girls got out their instruments and settled down for the rehearsal. Cassie's mind was racing – there was still so much to organise for their Gala. But soon, all was forgotten, as she concentrated on her violin part. She didn't know it that well that she dared take her eyes off the music.

The following night, Sunday, the members of the orchestra had substituted white blouses and black skirts (or white shirts and black trousers in the boys' case) for their normal uniforms. Some of their parents – the ones living in the Midlands particularly – had made a special effort to be there. Cassie and Emily were excited, knowing their fathers would both be in the audience.

They got ready in the vestry, waiting for the church to fill up. The girls both spotted their dads and smiled at them as they made their way down the aisle to the front of the church.

The orchestra started off the concert with two lively marches, and then it was Emily's first solo.

'Good luck!' Cassie mouthed at her, as she moved in front of the orchestra. The audience sat spellbound as the haunting sound of Emily's flute filled the church. Her second solo towards the end of the concert was, by contrast, fast and lively, but equally well received by the audience.

Emily's father rushed up to her at the end of the concert. Cassie was struck by how he had changed – gone was the pallor and anxiety from his face. He looked ten years younger.

'My darling girl!' he cried, hugging Emily. 'That was magical!' Cassie's dad came up then and the four of them had a good gossip about the latest Redwood news. Jake Brown gave his daughter a very proud smile when he heard all about the Gala.

'I'll put the date in my diary,' he said. 'By the way, I've got a date for you to remember – June 20th.'

'What's happening then?' asked Cassie.

'You've got an interview at the Reynard School for Girls in Shropshire, not far from home.'

Cassie tried to look enthusiastic.

'They have ballet, drama and music on the

curriculum,' he explained, 'but of course it won't be as high-powered as Redwood.'

'OK, Dad,' Cassie said, in a small voice.

Jake sighed. 'It's the best we can do, love. I'm sorry.'

Cassie decided there and then to try not to think about Reynard School for Girls until the day she had to go there for the interview. So much of her life was intertwined with Redwood – it would be very hard to let go.

The next morning, Cassie woke to the sound of someone crying. She forced her bleary eyes open and sat up. It was Emily.

'Whatever's the matter, Em?' she asked, hurriedly rolling out of bed and going across to her.

It took a few moments before Cassie could make any sense of what Emily, still convulsed with sobs, was trying to tell her.

But then Cassie saw for herself what had so upset her friend. Emily's flute lay on the bed before her – twisted and dented beyond repair.

'How's this happened?' asked Cassie, picking up the mangled instrument.

'Don't know,' sniffed Emily miserably. 'I just found it like this when I woke up.'

'Someone must have done it deliberately!' Cassie cried, looking about the bedroom. Becky and Poppy were still asleep. Abigail and Celia weren't there. Now that Yoko had left and Jane had gone on holiday, their room was not quite so crammed full as it had been when they'd first moved to the boys' block.

'It must have been Celia!' said Cassie. 'She was

pretty jealous about your flute solos, wasn't she?'

'An . . . and she wanted to dance the Rose in the Gala,' sobbed Emily. 'But how could she break my flute? I can't ask Mum and Dad to buy me a new one. They're only just getting back on their feet.'

'Perhaps the school will be able to lend you one,' Cassie suggested.

'But it won't be a good one like mine. It won't make a lovely sound!'

'Perhaps you could just manage for a while, till you can afford a new one. You've got the Gala and everything this term – dancing Cinderella as well. There's not going to be much time for playing your flute.'

'Oh, you don't understand, Cassie!' cried Emily. 'Music is so important to me now. I just can't live without it!'

'More important than dancing?' asked Cassie curiously.

'Yes, I think so,' Emily replied. 'When I leave Redwood, I'll probably have to go to an ordinary school, where they might not have good music tuition. But at least I can look for a good private flute teacher.'

'So ballet will go out of the window?' Cassie asked.

'I expect so,' said Emily. 'I know I'll miss it dreadfully, but if I have to choose between private lessons in ballet or flute, it'll be the flute every time.'

'Oh, if only Redwood weren't closing!' Cassie exclaimed. 'It's just going to mess up everything.'

Abigail and Celia came back into the room.

'Morning,' said Abigail. 'I've just had a lovely bath.

There aren't such queues if you get up early enough.' She noticed Emily's red-rimmed eyes and puffy face. 'What's the matter, Emily?' she asked.

Celia avoided looking in their direction as Cassie described what had happened, not only to Abigail but also to Poppy and Becky who were now awake. Cassie decided to confront Celia; she couldn't imagine who else would have done such a thing.

'Did you do it, Celia?' she demanded.

'No, of course not!' said Celia. A tell-tale redness flushed her cheeks.

Abigail turned to her. 'You were going on a lot about Emily last night, Celia. Are you quite sure you know nothing about it?'

Feeling the eyes of her room-mates all upon her, Celia's cheeks burned even more.

'It was you, wasn't it?' said Cassie.

Celia burst into tears. 'Don't report me!' she sobbed. 'I didn't mean it. I just got into such a terrible temper and I saw it lying there and stamped on it.'

'How could you!' Emily yelled. 'It's such a beautiful instrument and now you've ruined it!'

'I'm sorry,' said Celia. 'I'm really sorry, Emily. I was just so jealous of you. I don't know what came over me.'

'Being sorry won't give me my flute back!' cried Emily.

'I'll give you all my pocket money this term,' Celia promised, 'but please don't report me!'

For once, Cassie got the feeling that Celia really was ashamed of herself. Her anger over Emily's wrecked flute calmed down a little.

'I think we should wait and see before we do anything,' she said. 'If Celia can be a bit pleasanter to live with, perhaps we won't report her, not yet at least.'

'Oh, thank you!' cried Celia. 'I won't forget this. I promise I won't be so awful ever again.'

Their conversation was interrupted by a knock on the door. It was Miss Eiseldown.

'Morning, girls,' she said. 'Would you like to come to the hospital with me tonight, to visit Mrs Allingham? She's been asking her daughter about you, apparently.'

Cassie, Becky and Emily agreed to go, though it meant changing their rehearsal time to the lunch-hour.

'It's about time she was getting back on her feet,' said Cassie, as they fed the cats just after supper.

'Yes, it does seem to be taking ages,' said Becky. 'And Tinker and Marmalade do miss her so much.'

She stroked Tinker as Cassie and Emily quickly cleared up.

They ran back across to the school, where Miss Eiseldown was waiting for them in her car, on the front drive.

'Hop in,' she said. 'We won't have very long, but that's probably a good thing. We don't want to tire her out.'

It was weeks since the girls had been to see Mrs Allingham. Cassie felt a little guilty. There had just been so much to do and think about lately.

When they reached Mrs Allingham's ward, they saw that her daughter Emma was already sitting with her.

She and Miss Eiseldown went off to the coffee bar after a few minutes, so there wouldn't be too many visitors round the old lady's bed.

Mrs Allingham looked frail, but her face lit up when Cassie told her that the Gala performance of *Beauty and the Beast* was to be staged at the Birmingham Repertory Theatre.

'How exciting for you!' she said. 'And however sad you're feeling about Redwood having to close, you'll always have the memory of a special performance.'

'Perhaps you'll be able to get out of hospital in time to come and see it,' said Cassie.

A cloud passed over the old lady's eyes.

'We'll have to see,' she said. 'How are my cats?'

'They're fine,' Becky answered, 'but a bit lonely. Since Cassie's been calling so many rehearsals for the Gala, we only get time to feed them.'

'As long as they're well,' said Mrs Allingham. 'It's been a comfort to me knowing you'll look after them.'

Her daughter returned with Miss Eiseldown. 'You'd better leave her to rest now,' she said gently to the girls. Emma walked with them down the corridor a little way, after they had kissed Mrs Allingham goodbye.

'How have you girls enjoyed your time at Redwood?' Emma asked.

'It's been great,' Cassie answered for all of them. 'You were a student there too, weren't you?'

Emma laughed. 'It seems a long time ago now, but I loved it there. Never wanted to leave!'

Cassie went quiet. She was thinking of the time

when Poppy had stuck her foot through the attic floor when they were running the Unders and Overs race. Cassie had discovered the initial E.A. carved in a roof-joist and had often wondered whose they were. Could they have been Emma Allingham's?

'Did you ever carve your initials up in the attic?' she asked suddenly.

Emma looked at her in surprise. 'That must have been when we did the Unders and Overs!' she cried. 'I'd forgotten all about that!'

Cassie was pleased to have another mystery solved, but she came away from the hospital with the strong feeling that Mrs Allingham was growing weaker. The girls were so used to their friend being at Redwood, in her pretty little cottage. They had just thought it would only be a matter of time before she was back, as if nothing had changed.

Now, Cassie had a horrible vision of the cottage being bulldozed, along with the rest of the school buildings, to make way for an ugly new housing estate, while Mrs Allingham would have to spend the rest of her life in a hospital or nursing home. Cassie shuddered. The world she had known at Redwood seemed to be crumbling around her.

11

Sad News

Rehearsals got more frantic as the Gala drew closer, but Cassie was glad of all the extra work. She and Marianne had a great deal of organisation to do other than the actual dance production. Fortunately Madame was keen to help them and did all the necessary liaison with the theatre.

Mr Green gave Marianne over a hundred and fifty pounds from the ticket sales at their concert to spend on costumes and scenery. Madame put the girls in touch with Mrs Benbow, the dressmaker who often made the chief costumes for school productions.

The Beast's mask was a little more difficult. In the end, their art teacher, Miss Ryan, agreed to design and construct it from papier-mâché.

Some of the second and first years who weren't involved in the dancing were roped in to paint and make backdrops and scenery for the production, and Marianne got together a team of fourth years to collect the necessary props.

Soon, Mrs Benbow was coming to the school with tacked-up costumes. She was allowed the use of one of the smaller art rooms for fitting sessions with the principals.

Cassie was a little unsure about her own tutu, a scarlet velvet, criss-cross bodice with a white tulle skirt, and a scarlet travelling cloak for her journeys to and from the Beast's castle.

Marianne came with her for her second fitting.

'What do you think?' asked Cassie, giving a little twirl.

'Careful, dear,' warned plump Mrs Benbow in her rather throaty voice. 'It's only pinned and tacked!'

'I think it suits your dark hair wonderfully,' said Marianne. 'I thought it might.'

'It's more dramatic than pastel shades,' Mrs Benbow said, standing further back to admire her handiwork.

'Yes,' said Marianne. 'I didn't want it to look wishy-washy, or the Beast might have over-shadowed Beauty.'

'Oh, that would never do!' chuckled Mrs Benbow.

'What's Matthew wearing?' asked Cassie.

'Princely purple and white satin,' said Mrs Benbow.

'And whose is that pretty rose-pink tutu hanging up?'

'That's Emily's costume,' said Marianne. 'It's made all the difference having this money to spend!'

Cassie would really have preferred a prettier costume for herself, but understood that her character required a more dramatic one.

The two girls walked to the dining-hall together for supper.

'There's so much to think about, isn't there?' said Marianne. 'My head's spinning. When I lie down to go to sleep, I just keep thinking of things I've got to do for the Gala.'

'I know,' said Cassie. She had grown to like and respect the older girl very much. 'I hope it's not been too much of a burden for you.'

'Oh no, don't get me wrong. I'm enjoying every minute! We must give *Cinderella* another run through soon, to make sure no one's forgotten anything.'

'What about your friends' contemporary dance?' asked Cassie.

'They're practising it in their own time,' said Marianne. 'I had a look at it the other day and it's fine.'

'Good,' said Cassie. 'I'll nag Becky to get her tappers together again – it's a while since they went through their number.'

'I can't believe how smoothly rehearsals have gone lately!' exclaimed Marianne. 'Perhaps it's since Celia's been out of the way.'

'Could be,' said Cassie. 'Though actually she's fine in our room now. She's really tried hard to behave herself since the flute episode.'

'The flute!' exclaimed Marianne. 'I'd forgotten. Poor Emily.'

'Yes, she's still pretty upset about it. She doesn't know how she'll ever replace it.'

'That's really sad,' said Marianne. 'She plays so beautifully, doesn't she?'

'Yes,' agreed Cassie. 'I still don't know whether we've done the right thing in not reporting Celia. It was a dreadful thing to do.'

'Mmm, it must be difficult,' said Marianne, 'but at least you're getting a bit more sweetness and light in your dormitory. That's worth a lot.'

Cassie pondered Marianne's words as she ate her supper with Emily, Becky and Poppy.

'Are Celia's parents well off, do you think?' she asked them over supper.

'No idea,' said Emily. 'Why?'

'I wondered if you should write to them, letting them know what Celia did. Perhaps they would pay for a new flute?'

'I couldn't!' said Emily. 'I just couldn't.'

Cassie sighed. There didn't seem to be any other way to get a new instrument for her friend.

The next morning, when the girls went into ballet class, they noticed Miss Oakland had several slips of paper in her hand.

'I bet it's the results,' Cassie whispered to Emily.

She was right.

'The post has just arrived,' said Miss Oakland, 'so I thought you might like to hear your examination results straight away.'

Cassie hoped that she had done better than in her last exam. She waited nervously while the ballet mistress handed out slips to the girls who had taken the Elementary exam. Poppy was one of the first to receive hers. With a beaming smile, she told Cassie and Emily that she'd been highly commended.

Cassie and Emily had to wait till last. Cassie read her mark and jumped for joy.

'What did you get, Em?' she cried.

'Honours,' said Emily delightedly.

'Me too!' cried Cassie. 'I can't believe it!'

Miss Oakland was very pleased with the set of marks. 'Excellent work, girls,' she said, 'but don't think that means you can get lazy. Let's start with pliés at the barre, please. And in the centre, we'll work up to grands jetés en tournant.'

Miss Oakland's sessions on that particular jumping step always gave Cassie aching legs afterwards. But today she could have faced thirty-two fouettés, she was so happy!

Comparing marks after the lesson, Cassie soon discovered hers was the joint highest with Emily. She wondered if this might put her in the running for the Junior Shield, or if her last exam mark ruled her out. The Junior Shield was awarded annually at the end of the summer term to the outstanding girl dancer of the Junior section. Although it was open to first and second years, in practice it was always won by a second year.

It would be a fine thing to take away with me, thought

Cassie, but she knew that she had stiff competition from Emily and Abigail.

It was Saturday and a fine June day. The friends decided to walk into the village after lunch, to buy some cakes to celebrate their success.

'Can I help you celebrate?' asked Becky, who hadn't taken the exam.

'Of course you can.' said Cassie. 'It wouldn't be the same without you, Becky.'

'Oh, that's all right then,' said Becky, looking relieved.

Their first visit was to the cake shop, where they greedily selected chocolate eclairs and cream doughnuts.

'We'll have to get back quickly with these,' said Emily, 'or the cream will go off.'

The sun was becoming quite hot, as the morning haziness cleared. The girls walked briskly, glad they had had permission not to wear their blazers. As they passed the top of the avenue where the Blanes lived, Cassie glanced down it. She saw a car outside The Yews, with two men standing talking beside it.

'Hang on,' called Cassie, lingering behind her friends. 'Who have we here?'

The other three came back to her. 'Oh, Mr Smithson!' said Poppy.

'What's old sandy-hair doing here, I wonder?' said Cassie.

'Who's that with him?' asked Becky.

'It's the same man I saw him talking to one day in the village – the one with the droopy moustache. And if I'm not mistaken,' said Cassie, peering intently down the avenue, 'his name is Mr Blane.'

'Oh!' said Becky in surprise. 'Do you think so?'

'Wait,' said Cassie. 'They're just shaking hands. Mr Smithson's about to get into his car . . .'

'You're right,' said Becky. 'The moustache man is going into The Yews. He must be Mr Blane.'

'Come on, let's move,' said Cassie, 'before the surveyor drives his car past us!'

The more she thought about it, the more suspicious Cassie felt about Mr Blane, school trustee *and* property developer, being mixed up with Mr Smithson. After the cream cakes, Cassie aired her suspicions to her friends.

'We've got to keep a close eye on those two,' said Cassie. 'It shouldn't be too difficult.'

'Do we ever get time?' sighed Becky. 'Rehearsals seem to take up every minute.'

'We'll have to make time,' said Cassie. 'This could be really important.'

'I don't know how you find the energy,' sighed Becky. 'What I want to do now is curl up for a nice long nap.'

'What we need to find out,' said Cassie, 'is if Mr Blane has any connection at all with the plans for building on Redwood's land.'

'How can we do that?' asked Poppy.

'I'm not sure,' said Cassie, 'but I'll find a way.'

At supper, Cassie was still chewing over the problem when she noticed Miss Eiseldown walking across the dining-hall towards them. She seemed to be in a hurry.

'Girls,' she said, 'have you finished your supper? Yes? Would you come along to my room please, as soon as you've cleared your plates?'

The friends went to their house-mother's room, wondering what she wanted with them. None of them was at all prepared for what she had to tell them.

'Sit down, girls,' said Miss Eiseldown. 'I'm afraid I have some rather sad news for you.'

Thoughts of her family flitted through Cassie's mind; then she realised that all four of them wouldn't be there if that were so.

'I've just had news from Emma at the hospital. Mrs Allingham died peacefully in her sleep in the early hours of this morning.'

'Oh no!' cried Cassie. The others looked stunned.

'I know this must be terribly upsetting for you, but it was better for her that she went quickly and didn't have months and months of suffering.'

Cassie stared at the floor. It was the first time that a close friend had died. An empty feeling welled up inside her, as the tears streaked down her cheeks.

'Poor Tinker and Marmalade,' sobbed Becky. 'They'll miss her as much as we will!'

Cassie thought again how relentlessly things were changing: Redwood closing, the end of her ballet career and now the loss of a dear friend.

The friends wandered back towards the boys' block with sad thoughts.

'I don't feel like going to our room,' said Cassie, at the door of the block. 'Celia will be there. I couldn't face her at the moment.'

'Oh, she's been so much nicer to me!' said Emily. 'She's a different person.'

'I don't want to tell anyone else just yet,' Cassie explained. 'Let's go to the folly. We'll be on our own there.'

'It'll only make us feel worse, seeing her cottage,' Poppy remarked.

'But we've got to feed the cats anyway,' Becky pointed out.

They sat in the ruin, talking over all their memories of Mrs Allingham.

'Do you remember when we first spied her cottage from here?' said Cassie. 'It was so exciting finding a little house at the edge of the grounds.'

'And how we used to garden for her,' added Becky.

'And how that horrible antiques man tried to trick her into giving him her lovely poppies painting,' said Emily.

'None of us could have guessed it would turn out to be so valuable,' Cassie added.

Becky looked at her watch. 'The cats will be hungry,' she said.

No one moved. It was going to be hard to visit the cottage now. Becky stood up. 'Come on,' she said. 'Let's get it over with.'

The girls went through the copse and steeled themselves to enter Mrs Allingham's garden. The cats rushed up to them as they approached.

'They know something's wrong,' said Emily. 'Cats are supposed to be psychic.'

'I guess they're just plain hungry,' said Becky, giving Tinker a stroke.

The cottage looked as pretty as ever; the cleaner had been coming regularly to keep it in good order. As the girls went in, they could almost hear the silence. Cassie thought the house felt emptier and quieter than ever.

Perhaps the house knows too, thought Cassie. *Perhaps it's been waiting, like the cats, and now they all know she's not coming back.*

'I feel strange,' said Emily. She was obviously sensing something similar to Cassie. She shivered. 'Do you mind if I wait outside in the sun?'

'No, go on, Emily,' said Becky. 'We won't be long.'

Cassie was beginning to find the cottage oppressive too and joined Emily outside.

'It's like a whole portion of our lives has ended,' said Emily, gazing at the roses blooming at the door.

'I know just how you feel,' said Cassie. 'I can't bear it.'

'Will you stay my friend, after we've left Redwood?' Emily asked quietly.

'Of course I will,' said Cassie. 'We'll see each other in the holidays. It'll be just like old times.'

But Cassie knew as she said it that it wouldn't ever be the same again.

The next few days passed quite miserably, although the girls couldn't allow themselves to have any time off from their Gala rehearsals.

On Thursday, Miss Wrench sent for them after breakfast.

'Mrs Allingham's solicitor has been in touch with me,' explained Miss Wrench, 'about the contents of her will. June was very upset at the idea of Redwood closing down – as we all are – and she has left a major part of her estate, thirty thousands pounds in all, to the school. Unfortunately, you know the estimated cost of repairs is way above that figure, so her money will be useless.'

She sighed. 'I shall find a suitable charity. But now we come to her bequests to you girls.'

The friends looked at one another in bewilderment.

'I'll read what she actually wrote:

For my Redwood friends, in gratitude and friendship, I bequeath to Poppy, my amethyst brooch. To Rebecca, my dear cats, Tinker and Marmalade, as I know she'll find them a good home. To Emily, my flute, in the hope she will carry on with her music-making, and to Cassandra, my wardrobe of costumes, for I know she will treasure them as I have.'

Cassie felt a strong tug of affection for the old lady, as Miss Wrench read out the bequests. It wasn't until the next day that it came home to any of them the value of what they'd been given.

That evening they were due to go home for the weekend, apart from Poppy, who was going to Becky's house. Just before their parents came to collect them, Mrs Allingham's daughter invited them over to the cottage.

'Poppy and I can take the cats now,' said Becky enthusiastically. 'Dad will be here in a minute.'

'Don't you think you should check with your parents first?' asked Emma.

'No, I know it will be fine,' said Becky. 'Mum loves cats and it's like a zoo already at our house.'

Poppy was delighted with her brooch, which was made in the shape of a star. 'It was a thoughtful present,' she said, 'for someone like me who has to travel light.'

Emily's flute caused her great excitement. She couldn't resist taking it out of the case and playing it in the cottage.

'It has such a beautiful tone!' she cried. 'It's even better than my old one!'

'My mother told me what a good player you are,' said Emma, with a smile. She opened up the wardrobe of costumes and Cassie experienced again the thrill of seeing and touching the old lady's lovely garments.

'There's no rush to clear them out.'

'I'll ask my dad when he comes,' said Cassie. 'There might be room in the car.'

Fortunately, Cassie was only taking home a weekend bag and her violin, so she and her father laid the costumes carefully on the back seat.

'I'll have to build another wardrobe for these,' said Jake.

Emma laughed. 'I know Cassie will have hours of pleasure trying them on.'

'I'll never part with them!' Cassie cried. 'And they'll always remind me of Mrs Allingham!'

12

A Hiding Place

After Mrs Allingham's funeral, Cassie thought often about the old lady's words to her about fighting for the school. Wonderful as the costumes were, perhaps her words were the true legacy she left to Cassie.

All the costumes had been stored at home, with the exception of one really lovely primrose-yellow dress, which she brought back with her to Redwood. It was calf-length, with a full net skirt and a sequinned satin bodice with short puffed sleeves. It was just the kind of dress she imagined Beauty wearing after she had gone to live at the Beast's castle. She was relieved to find that Marianne agreed with her.

Cassie hadn't let up a bit on her rehearsal

programme for the Gala. All the items were coming on nicely, though *Beauty and the Beast* still needed the most work.

'I've seen Mr Smithson snooping about again,' Cassie said to her friends, one lunch-time, about a week after the funeral.

'Is it really worth watching him?' Becky asked. 'I don't know about you, but I'm exhausted with all this rehearsing.'

'It's Saturday,' said Cassie. 'We've got at least a couple of hours before our rehearsal.'

'I know,' said Becky, but I've got so behind with my school work. I'll have to spend the afternoon catching up.'

Cassie knew that Becky had got very absorbed in a science project and probably wanted to continue working on it. Poppy had already arranged to go to the village.

'What about you, Em?' Cassie asked.

'I'm free,' she replied. 'What do you want us to do?'

'Just shadow him – get a good idea of what he's doing.'

Cassie had last seen the surveyor near the girls' wing, so the two friends made their way to it. They soon had him in their sights, and flattened themselves against a wall, so they wouldn't be seen.

He didn't seem to be doing anything in particular. He had no measuring tape or instruments with him. Every few minutes he checked his watch, and paced up and down, looking about him.

'He seems to be waiting for someone,' whispered Cassie.

Sure enough, a few minutes later they saw the man with the moustache, who they now knew to be Mr Blane, walking briskly across the grounds towards him.

'He hasn't come from the front entrance,' whispered Emily. 'He must have come through the wicket gate by Mrs . . . the cottage.'

Emily swallowed. She couldn't call it Mrs Allingham's cottage any longer. Cassie squeezed her arm. Memories of their old friend were still painful.

'Perhaps he didn't want to be seen,' Cassie hissed.

The men almost immediately went into the back door of the wing.

'He must have unlocked it,' said Cassie. 'Come on, let's follow.'

'I don't know,' said Emily. 'It'll be harder to stay out of their way inside. I don't like that Mr Smithson.'

'We'll be careful,' said Cassie. She crept round the edge of the wing, checking each window before passing it. Emily followed her into the back entrance. In the lobby they stood motionless, listening intently.

'They're upstairs,' whispered Cassie. They moved noiselessly up the staircase and came on to the landing cautiously, but there was no sign of the two men. They listened again. The men's voices drifted towards them from the far end of the landing.

The girls stole towards the far rooms, but as they reached about halfway, Mr Blane suddenly appeared in a doorway. Fortunately, he had his back to the girls, as he was talking to Mr Smithson. This gave them the opportunity to dart into the nearest room, but the girls could hear footsteps coming towards them. The door stood open; to close it would attract attention, and it was unlikely they would actually come in the room, so Cassie considered hiding behind the door. Then it dawned on her – they were standing in Miss Oakland's old room. The room with the secret panel!

She yanked Emily across the room, pushed the trick panel and pulled her into the tiny hiding-place. From the inside, they quickly pushed the panel back into place, plunging themselves into total darkness.

'I hope we can open it again,' whispered Emily, who was trembling violently.

It was lucky they had hidden; the men presently wandered into Miss Oakland's room. From the other end of the landing, the friends had been unable to discover what the men were talking about, but now they could hear every word clearly.

'It's all going to happen, don't worry.'

'But won't they smell a rat when we don't actually knock the place down?'

'No. They'll just think we've done the necessary underpinning and spent a fortune on it, to turn it into luxury apartments.'

'I hope you're right. We stand to make a fortune through this little enterprise. There'll be the apartments and all the houses I can build in the grounds. If we can sell them, of course.'

'We'll sell them. A location like this – wonderful setting, just outside Birmingham. They'll be snapped up!'

'I still can't believe we'll get away with it. Are you

sure the old battleaxe doesn't suspect anything?'

Mr Smithson laughed. 'Not a thing.'

In the tight, dark confines of the secret hiding-place, Cassie squeezed Emily's hand. They both knew that the conversation they had overheard was to have tremendous importance not only to the ballet school, but to their own lives and careers.

The men were moving out of earshot, but the girls had heard enough. Emily was still trembling, and now Cassie felt a terrific surge of excitement and relief. Redwood's problems were about to be solved!

'Let's go and see the Wrench,' she said.

As soon as the two men were out of the way, the girls hurried down to the door leading to the main building, which was bolted on their side. They drew the bolts and stepped out into the busy corridor, then Cassie saw Miss Wrench walking quickly along the corridor towards them.

'Oh dear,' she said to Emily, 'we've found her a bit *too* quickly.'

'What have you two been doing in that wing again?' she said sharply. 'This is the second time you've disobeyed me!'

'Please, Miss Wrench,' Cassie began, 'we've got something very, VERY important to tell you and there's not a moment to lose!'

The Principal agreed to listen to their explanation in her study. When they had finished, all traces of anger had disappeared from her face.

'Thank you, Cassandra. Thank you, Emily. You have stumbled upon something which could well mean I shall be seeing you here again next term!' She beamed at them.

'What will you do, Miss Wrench?' asked Cassie.

'First, I shall phone the police. Second, I shall call in an independent team of surveyors.'

The friends learned the next day from Miss Eiseldown, that the new surveyors had found traces of subsidence only in the girls' wing. The main building was perfectly sound. The cost of repair would easily be met by Mrs Allingham's bequest.

'And what's going to happen to Mr Smithson and Mr Blane?' asked Cassie.

'They've both been arrested,' said Miss Eiseldown, 'and charged with fraud. They'll go to prison for it, I have no doubt.'

'So Redwood's saved?'

'Redwood's saved.'

The last couple of weeks of June zipped by at a tremendous pace. There was an overwhelming feeling of exhilaration and relief: the ballet school was to remain open! But the girls who were involved in the Gala didn't have a moment's rest.

Their dress rehearsal at the Birmingham Repertory four days before the performance was a bit of a disaster. Madame who had accompanied them, gave them all a pep-talk afterwards.

'Do not be dismayed mes chères,' she said. 'All is not lost. There is a saying: "A bad dress rehearsal makes a good first night!" I will help you back at school to iron out the difficulties you are 'aving.'

Madame was as good as her word. The problems which had shown up in *Beauty and the Beast* were owing to Marianne's inexperience at directing, as much as anything. Changing a few positions of entrances and exits and making a little more time for costume changes made all the difference to the production. On the day before their performance, it was running like clockwork.

'Oh, I'm so nervous,' said Cassie, that night, before bed. 'I know I won't sleep a wink.'

'What are you worrying about?' asked Becky.

'Well for a start,' said Cassie, 'if I slip, there'll be hundreds of people watching!'

'You won't slip,' Becky scoffed. 'You dance the part of Beauty as if you've known it all your life.'

'Isn't it funny,' said Poppy, smiling, 'we can think ahead now to next term. I could have been packing my bags for Australia in a few weeks!'

'And the Reynard School for Girls will never know what they missed!' laughed Cassie.

'We'll be third years,' said Becky. 'Seniors! Can you believe it!'

Cassie grabbed Becky's hands and led her in a wild sort of dance round the room.

'We'll wear buns, not plaits!' she yelled.

'And dark blue leotards!' cried Becky.

'And tights, not socks!'

'And go to bed at *nine* o'clock!'

'That rhymes!' screeched Cassie, collapsing on the floor, with Becky half on top of her.

'I thought you were nervous!' said Emily. 'Have you got your costumes ready?'

'I've hung mine on the wardrobe door, look!' said Cassie.

'It's a beautiful dress, that yellow one!'

'I know,' said Cassie. 'It's lovely to dance in, too. And, I know it sounds silly, but it sort of makes me feel that Mrs Allingham's there with me on stage, willing me to dance well.'

'I always think about her when I play my flute,' said Emily.

'Have you forgiven me yet?' asked Celia, sheepishly, from her bed in the corner.

'Yes, I've forgiven you,' said Emily. 'Everything turned out all right in the end, didn't it?'

'Well, I got you a little present, anyway,' said Celia, looking embarrassed. 'To try and make amends and to bring you good luck tomorrow.'

To Emily's surprise, she handed her a parcel. Inside was a good luck charm – a shiny, rather brash horseshoe on a chain.

'Oh – er – thank you,' said Emily. 'I'm sure it'll bring me luck.'

'Good luck to all you guys,' said Celia, smiling.

Abigail grinned at her. 'Thanks, Celia. We'll probably need it.'

Whether it was the good luck charm, or just the culmination of a lot of hard work, the Gala performance was a brilliant success.

The extracts from *Cinderella*, the tap sequence and the contemporary number made up the first half, with the second devoted to *Beauty and the Beast*.

Cassie had never felt quite so nervous before. She

was conscious that it was a full house, and that her own family was out there in the auditorium. Thankfully, a sea of faces in front of her blurred into an amorphous mass of colours.

She knew Emily had done extremely well as Cinderella, receiving three curtain calls before the interval. Conscious that there would be comparisons, Cassie put everything she'd got into her portrayal of Beauty. She had to put over Beauty's bravery in offering to go to the Beast's castle, to save her father's life, her initial fear at meeting the Beast and her growing tenderness and affection for him.

It was as though the part had been made especially for her. Cassie could identify with Beauty at every stage of the story. An older dancer could not have portrayed her innocence so convincingly.

The audience loved her! She sensed it after her final pas de deux with the Beast, now revealed as the Prince. And she was quite sure of it when a roar of applause met her ears at the end of the ballet.

She and Emily were both presented with lovely sprays of flowers; pink carnations for Cassie and red roses for Emily. Then, the cast were invited to remain on stage, while Miss Wrench said a few words to the audience.

'This is not a school Gala,' she said, 'in the ordinary sense. It has been produced by the students whose names appear on the programme.'

There was an instant rustling of paper.

'You will wonder, therefore, why I am giving a speech. Well, firstly, I wish to thank and congratulate all the girls and boys who have made this evening a resounding success . . .'

Here there was more thunderous applause.

'. . . and secondly, to let the world know, if there can be any doubt in anyone's mind, that Redwood Ballet School is alive and kicking and looking ahead to a long and successful future!'

'Finally, it is my great pleasure to award some special prizes to members of the cast. Most prizes will be given out as usual on Speech Day at the end of term, but I wanted to take this, more public opportunity, to reward some of the students who not only have shown their ability as dancers, but also have helped to save their school!'

Cassie and Emily exchanged glances. They hadn't been expecting this!

'Rebecca Hastings,' called Miss Wrench and Becky duly scurried to the front of the stage, 'receives a brand new prize, The Tap Dancing Trophy.'

Becky curtseyed and took the cup with a rather embarrassed grin on her face.

'Emily Pickering,' Miss Wrench announced, 'for excellent progress, despite the setback of an illness, another new prize, The Allingham Cup.'

Emily looked as if she didn't know whether to laugh or cry as she received her award.

'And finally, to our most outstanding Junior girl student, Cassandra Brown, we should like to present the Junior Shield!'

Cassie took the shield in a daze, only remembering to curtsey at the last moment. She stood between her two friends, Becky and Emily, and faced the audience, who were clapping once more. On an impulse, she raised the Shield above her head, cheers from the cast behind ringing in her ears.

Memories from her days at Redwood raced through her mind. Mrs Allingham's cottage. The ghost which had haunted the Ballet School. Mitsi, their homesick friend from Japan. Emily's illness and disappearance. The tour of France. And now this.

There had been good moments and bad, triumphs and disappointments. But throughout the two years, Cassie had always held on to the driving ambition of her life. To be a dancer.